About the Author

A.B. Kyazze is a British–American writer and photographer. She spent two decades writing and taking photographs around the world in conflicts and natural disasters – in Africa, Asia and Southern Europe. Her photographs and non-fiction work have been published in travel magazines, *The Huffington Post*, *The Washington Times*, *The International Review of the Red Cross,* and by Oxfam, Save the Children, the British Red Cross, and the Humanitarian Practice Network of the Overseas Development Institute. She also writes short stories and book reviews and teaches creative writing workshops for children. Today, she lives in southeast London with her young family. *Into the Mouth of the Lion* is her first novel.

Into the Mouth
of the Lion

A.B. Kyazze

unbound

This edition first published in 2021

Unbound

TC Group, Level 1, Devonshire House, One Mayfair Place, London W1J
8AJ

www.unbound.com

ISBN (eBook): 978-1-78965-114-0
ISBN (Paperback): 978-1-78965-113-3

Cover design by Mecob

Printed and bound in Great Britain by Clays Ltd, Elcograf S.p.A.

Super Patrons

Jin Ah Bellefuil
Tuikku Alaviitala
Katherine Anderson
Vicki Ashmore
Lois Austin
Family Baker
Marc Balsys
Elizabeth Barry
Gweneth Barry
Pat Barry
Alex Bell
Tam Bellefuil
Lisa Bense
Andrea and Adam Berg
Maria Vittoria Beria
Gaela Bernini
Marianne Bick–Schwab
Daniella Bleu
Edmund Blok
Helen Blythsmith
Andrew Bonwick

Fred and Ede Bookstein
Torey Bookstein
Lisa Bookstein & Ken Bloom
Rachel Booth
Liana Bruce
Michael Burrows & Kate Allum
Zia Choudhury
Dale Chu
Graham Conlon
Peter Cordwell
Debra Courville
Pasquale D'Arbela
Dileeni Daniel-Selvaratnam
Stijn De Lameillieure
Matthew de Lange
James Dickinson
Paul Elevique
Lisa Ellis
Alyson Eynon
Anne Falchi
Ang-Mitchell Family
Jessica Faul
Matthew Feldman
Catherine Fitzgibbon
Victoria Flint
Julie Fritts
Norman Frost
Shereen George
Catherine Godin
Julia Golding
Jean-Michel Grand
Deborah Haines
Monica Hand

Ellen Harland
Veronica Harris
Marc Harrison
Kelly Harry
Annie Hawes
Marilyn Huckans
Anne Jacobs
Nev Jefferies
Clea Kahn
Cyprian Kibuka
Katie Kibuuka
Agnieszka Kiona
Sylvia Kizito
Calie & Peter Koso
Sofia, Eliza and Lindsay Koso
Christine Kyazze
Goobi Kyazze
Kanatta Kyazze
Mimi Kyazze
Emmanuelle Lacroix
Nicole Lanouette
Marc-henry Lebrun
Grey Lee
Marcus Lenzen
Joanna Lofthouse
David MacDonald
Natasha Marhia
Barbara Marsh
Biram Mboob
Bridget McGechie
Alan McLeod
Aidan McQuade
Hema Mistry

Anne Mortensen
Marsha Mumm
Rike Nieländer & Stefan Halberstadt
Sanyu Ntanda
Sorcha O'Callaghan
Kerrie O'Connor
Michael O'Donnell
Glenn Olarte
Kym Ormay
Helen Palmer
Andrea Parkanska
Sarah Patten
Melanie Pennant
Sophie Plagerson
Leah Plunkett
Briana Pobiner
Caitlin Porter
Alice Portuphy
Jeff Ragusa
Ash Ray
Oliver Ray
Samuel Renard
James Reynolds
Ebony Riddell Bamber
Nick Roseveare
Philomena Roulland
Abby Rowe
Danielle Safran
Carolyn Seabury
Kim Segel
Jay Shah
Tish Shah
Julia Silk

Daniel Sinnathamby
Michelle Smith
Flora Spiegel
Emily Steadman
Rose Stevens
Jane Sturtridge
Ami Sugar
Gail & Alan Sugar
Sophia Swithern
Pam Takhar
Inga & Philippe Tenhaeff
Gilles Thal Larsen
Joe Thomas
Bea Thombs
Stewart Twidle
John Harlan Underhill
Misha Vaswani
Katy Webley
Amanda Weisbaum
Natacha Weiss
Terri Wills
Matt Wingate
John H Wood
Sophie Zunz

Prologue

The Angolan civil war lasted for twenty-six years – with some interludes of calm – from 1975 until 2002. The conflict pitted the People's Movement for the Liberation of Angola (MPLA – the de facto government led by José Eduardo dos Santos) against the National Union for the Total Independence of Angola (UNITA – the rebels, led by Jonas Savimbi).

The country served as a Cold War battleground. The United States and the Soviet Union supported opposing sides and used mercenaries from South Africa, Cuba and many other places. The MPLA profited from the discovery of oil in offshore reserves, while UNITA paid for arms and ammunition with smuggled diamonds, known as 'blood diamonds'.

Journalists and human rights groups published the facts, making it clear that the selling of these blood diamonds fuelled the insurgency and prolonged the fighting. There were calls for international investigations, and UN sanctions were placed against anyone who knowingly traded in diamonds from rebel-held parts of the country.

At the conflict's height, about 3.8 million people were displaced, one-third of the population, living like refugees in their own country. There were some 90,000 amputees, mainly from landmine accidents and war wounds. The child survival rate was such that one child in three would not reach the age of five.

Part I

One

City of Malanje, Angolan Highlands, end of January 2002

You are thrown backwards by the blast, out of the shack, stumbling and falling.

'Maria!' you scream as you scramble back up. You're clawing your way to the doorway. Inside it is black with orange fragments of flame, spread in a circle.

The smoke pricks your eyes and you cover your mouth and nose with the collar of your shirt. You are crying and shouting at the same time. You smell burnt hair and an awful wet human scent that you've never known before.

'Maria, where are you, Maria?'

You hear voices outside, people who heard the explosion.

You have to get away from there. From that burnt destructive air. Can't breathe, can't speak. The breath is screeching in your tightened throat. Your ears pulse with your heartbeat, pounding you into submission and acceptance of this new state. She's gone. But no, can't be. Impossible.

The commotion around you is a roar of concerned people trying to put out the flames. They are a blur of silhouettes and shadows, faces occasionally coming into focus and intruding. Well-meaning, too late. She's gone.

You don't care about the house, the fire, the damage. It was your home, but they are all brittle pieces of nothing, now that she is no longer there. You push back, standing up awkward and fast. 'Sorry,' is all you can manage as you step on someone's foot, or something else in your way.

You shield your face from everyone. As long as no one looks you in the eye, you can possibly hold it together. Won't fall to pieces, not just yet.

They won't know what's going on inside your head. Won't connect the dots. Won't step forward to stop you.

It was meant for you, you know it's true. They got the wrong target. An innocent woman, killed.

The starting gun has fired and you are off.

No explanation.

No plan.

Two

Luanda, Angola, February 2002

Salão de para partidas domésticas. Lena makes her way to the domestic departures hall. The fluorescent lights buzz loudly, throwing off a green hue. There is no glass in the windows, and the frames are twisted and abandoned. Outside, a small plane sits where it crashed years before, nose bent up by the impact. Red dust covers all the surfaces and hovers in the air.

As Lena sits and waits, she looks at the passport in her hand. The document is British, with a Portuguese name: *Magdalena Gloria Rodrigues.* English speakers always get it a bit wrong. Her first name doesn't sound like 'leaning'; she has always been known as Lena, pronounced like the sound in 'rain'. Maybe in Angola, where Portuguese is more widely spoken, they'll get it right.

She catches her hand shaking. She slips it under her leg to steady herself.

Around her, there is a cluster of Angolan nuns, faces shaded under simple white habits. Other people are harder to categorise. Two European women wearing khaki vests talk over a laptop. An Angolan man in a dark suit sits with a briefcase and a small duffle bag at his feet. A white man, wearing a broad safari-type hat, sits with his legs splayed out, taking up too much space.

A long-legged man with sunglasses and greasy blond hair walks past. 'I don't know if we'll make it, but I suppose I'll try,' he says to no one in particular.

She looks around to see if anyone else has heard. Two of the nuns quickly cross themselves. The man strides through security and it occurs to her that he could be the pilot.

An announcement scratches over the PA system. Even though Portuguese is her mother tongue, she recognises nothing in the stream of words except her destination: 'Malanje'. The strangers stand up and gather their belongings. The nuns brush off some of the red dust; the others don't bother. They all make their way down to a creaking old security scanner.

On the tarmac, an aged propeller plane awaits. It looks impossibly small to fly, but it seems to be the plane for the highlands. The passengers put their luggage directly in the underbelly and then climb up unsteady stairs into the body of the plane.

She chooses a seat by a window. Two nuns sit across from her, quickly fastening flimsy seat belts. The nun closest to her is plump and seems uncomfortable on the small seat. She turns to Lena and shows a bright grin, eyebrows lifting up in expectation. A gold cross hangs around her neck.

'Are you all right, dear?' the nun asks.

She nods, too fast. 'Absolutely fine. It's my mum who was afraid of flying, not me. She never would have got on this plane.'

The nun gives a gentle smile, feigning belief.

The man with sunglasses and greasy hair is indeed the pilot. He has to duck his head as he strides through the small cabin. He reaches out to pull the door shut from the inside. He gives a half-hearted recital of a safety lecture. The sunglasses are lowered to give a glance to each row and each seat-belted lap. He seems satisfied as he launches himself back into the cockpit. It takes extra effort to fold his long legs into place.

'You won't need air masks,' he says. 'This plane can't fly that high.'

The engines start up. A member of the ground crew gives a thumbs-up and steps back. The plane pivots, bumps towards the runway, then speeds towards take off.

She grips the armrest and tries to focus on her breath. She tells herself to trust the pilot. No choice. One hand goes up instinctively to the St Christopher's necklace from her mum. She always has it around her neck for protection.

The noise and vibration crowd out everything else. The plane lifts and the vibration changes when the wheels are no longer in contact with the solid ground. There is a moment when she feels her breath is lifting too, and helping to carry them. Then the plane surprises her by banking sharply to the left as it heads eastwards.

Out of the oval window, the coastline of Luanda arcs away. Heat shimmers off tin shanty-town roofs from the vast slums. Sleek luxury apartments rise up in towers of grandeur, ignoring the spread of squalor below. It is a very dusty urban scene, with no green to be seen, except the emerald ocean moving into the distance. Rusty red is the overwhelming colour – the soil, the bricks of the buildings, the haze which refuses to settle.

With bumps and jerks, they continue the ascent. The city is quickly behind them and low mountains unfold roughly ahead. Unassertive hill tracks are visible, void of vehicles. The shadow of the plane races along the ground in the late afternoon sun.

She tries to see if she can recognise any military installations, but none are in sight. She takes out her camera and starts to compose a picture. The dirt on the glass and the awkward angle would make it a mediocre shot at best. She soon gives up and rests it on her lap, turned off. It is reassuring to have something to hold onto. She rubs her thumb over the familiar dials and switches, and squints at the horizon. The dark reds and browns blur and blend like a watercolour.

DJ, where the hell have you gone?

She doesn't know where to start to guess DJ's moves, thoughts or motivations. Her sister – eight years older – has been abroad for more than ten years. And even when DJ was visiting London between missions, she was an enigma.

DJ didn't want to be figured out or labelled, especially not by family. Lena knew from their friends and from watching others that Portuguese families were traditionally supposed to be tightly knit and close. Perhaps that was what Mum and Dad hoped for, and why they so often seemed disappointed. DJ rebelled against expectations, and the family was not strong enough to hold her in.

DJ never felt the obligation to explain her activities or absences. There must have been photographs, but not many were shared to give a sense of destination or even of direction of travel. That was DJ.

Lena was different. She watched her sister's choices, but she didn't feel the same urgency to break free. She travelled a little, in the summer before Uni and that time in Portugal when there was a gap between contracts. But she never felt the drive that she saw in others, something edgy pushing them to get out.

In London, she found her satisfaction in noticing the things that others might miss in their rush. Photography was the way she approached the world. The light was what she always saw first. It hit her wherever she went – the quality of the light and the effect as it danced across a scene or left important corners in shadow. On good days, photography provided her with the chance to focus all her energy and intention on the perfect shot. She was much more comfortable living in the background, taking photographs, keeping to herself. That had been the way since Dad died four years ago, with Mum following soon afterwards. It was easier to avoid making plans or having lofty ambitions. That was how it was, until now.

'I forgot to tell you!' the pilot shouts out over his shoulder. 'The landing is a bit difficult! The rebels have surface-to-air missiles, so I can't bring us in gradually. I have to stay high then circle around tight over Malanje. You'll feel the G-force strongly, but it shouldn't hurt.' He makes more of an effort to look back at the passengers. 'Anybody have a heart problem?'

They look at each other, wide-eyed.

'Good!' he says, and presses the engines forward.

Ahead, a settlement rises into view. Not a city, more like a frontier town coming out of the bleak landscape. When the plane gets closer, the engine noise comes down a notch and lights flash from the cockpit. Then the plane tips sharply right and goes into a downward spiral.

She feels the plane accelerate towards the ground. She is pinned to her seat with the feeling of an immense weight against her chest. She can't move. She can't blink, she can barely breathe.

Then, somehow, the pilot knows when to straighten out. The plane lands with a bump on a dirt airstrip. The passengers are thrown forward as the engines roar to slow it down. But it all settles quickly. Except for her heart and her breathing. She consciously tries to calm her body, but the alarms are still hammering inside her long after the plane comes to a stop.

She looks across at the nuns. They look astonished and grateful. She turns back to the other passengers and their faces are harder to read. They seem unflustered, as if this spiral landing was normal and expected in this kind of place.

The propellers roll to a halt followed by a silence that leaves an empty feeling in her ears. The pilot crosses the plane with three strides and opens the door with a crunch of the seal being released. He seems happy with himself, and pleasantly surprised, that he's managed to dodge the missiles again – this time.

Three

London, six days earlier

'They wouldn't tell me everything that happened.' Lena sank into Lucien's deep sofa. The flat, shared with his brothers, stank of lager and yesterday's fish and chips. The place was damaged by too many parties where the end of the night was a blur or a fight or both. She was used to how it felt to be there, like borrowing a friend's coat to run to the shops to get cigarettes.

Her heart was beating too fast and she chewed on her fingernails. There was a taste of grime in her mouth that made her want to spit, but there was nowhere to let it go.

'What have they told you, then?' Lucien asked, holding himself more than an arm's length away from her.

'They won't tell me anything, not really. Just asked me to hang on and wait.'

'How can they not fucking tell you? Your own sister. That's rubbish.'

'There was some accident. DJ was involved in it but not hurt. There's a police investigation. And now she's gone missing.'

He exhaled loudly.

'I tried to tell them that I should come,' she continued, 'to be there for her. But they didn't listen. Didn't understand.'

'Fucking rubbish.'

She looked over at him. He was her faithful childhood friend. He stuck by her, even through the awkward times that came with someone you used to sleep with, but didn't any more. He knew her, so well. He was so at ease in this space, in London. He'd always been here. He never understood DJ's need to get out.

'I gotta get there, you know?' she said. 'She's my sister. If something happens to her, I've got no one else.'

'But isn't it dangerous? A bloody civil war or something?'

'That's no reason not to go. DJ's been living there for years, nothing's happened to her until now. They're just telling me to wait…'

'But you don't want to.'

'What good does that do? No fucking good at all.' She felt an urgent need to move. She started to walk the lengths of the floorboards back and forth, kicking things out of the way.

'And it's not like there's anything holding me here in London. Can't even afford a place to sleep, since the bloody bank took everything that Dad staked on the business. There's nothing for me here, just your stupid couch,' she said.

'Don't be rude; that couch has supported you a lot over the years.'

She went over to him from behind and rubbed his shoulders. His aftershave, as always, permeated the air all around him. 'I know, mate, truly I do. Don't be angry. You know I love you and your couch.'

He didn't look at her, but his shoulders relaxed a little. 'It's not my fault you spent your last penny on that digital camera contraption.'

'No, not your fault. I accept all responsibility for that one.'

'So, what are you gonna do?'

'I need to go, try to help. I could be the one to find her, you know. Despite what you think, we're connected like that.'

'But she hasn't come back to see you in, like… forever? Since she was such a bitch at your mum's funeral.'

She dropped her hands from his shoulders, hated that memory. 'People behave badly after a death; everyone knows that.'

'I'm just saying, what has she done for you lately?'

'She sends postcards sometimes…'

'Holiday snaps?'

'I got one last month, remember? From her trip to South Africa over Christmas.'

'That's it? That's your justification to go into a war zone?'

'You don't get it, do you? Call it women's intuition.'

'Right. You think that applies to DJ?'

'Don't be an arse. I need your help on this.'

He turned to look at her. 'Heard that before. What do you need?'

'Your skills, on the laptop.'

Eleven Belgrave Square. A faded sign announced: *Emergency visas for lusophone African countries can be obtained with the proper forms and arriving no later than half-past two.* Lena's place in the queue advanced slowly, about one person called every ten minutes. Time to think. Too much time.

She wondered if she should've broken that contract. Might be a long time before the next pay cheque, and her overdraft was feeling the pain of this international flight. Would DJ have done the same for her? Not sure.

But she couldn't just sit back and wait. She had to find her sister, to make sure she was okay.

She noted the CCTVs in the corner, one aimed at the door,

the other at the front of the queue. There was a *No Cameras* sign above the clerk's head, behind bullet-proof glass. If she had been allowed her camera, what would she capture? The woman pulling at the hem of her plum-coloured coat, not seeing the ladder starting to break through the weak fabric. Other people, lined with soft sadness, were waiting expectantly but not necessarily hopeful. No, emergency visas were not for good news. Not for honeymoons or sunny package holidays. They were simply a way to respond to grim events as required.

On the phone, DJ's boss Mr Appiah had spoken in a quiet voice with a West African accent. He had seemed so calm, but it was hard to tell what kind of man he was, over the line. There had been an accident and a fire, he'd said. One local staff member had been tragically killed, and he was busy dealing with that. DJ had taken off the same evening, without official permission. It had been a few days and now she was considered a missing person. They were calling Lena as she was listed as next-of-kin, following the proper procedure after a traumatic incident.

'Traumatic? Then maybe I should come out there, to help her,' she'd said.

'Well no, you see, that could be a problem.' He had seemed to lose track of what he'd been saying. 'It's very dangerous, and you've got no training. In a conflict environment, you need to follow certain protocols, or you could be a risk to yourself and the team.' He'd lost her in the list of regulations. She had hung up the phone in despair.

But now, in the visa office, thanks to Lucien and his forged letter – not half-bad – with the letterhead from the desk of one Kojo Appiah himself, Country Director of Community Water Angola (CWA), it might just work out.

Four

The light is much brighter and harsher than Lena expects – the grey of London's February is far away. The heat hits her like an invisible wave and makes her feel unsure and unsteady.

A line of Angolan drivers, families, well-wishers and street-sellers are pressed up against a rusty metal fence that does not look like it has any strength left. A cluster of well-dressed women, wearing fresh lipstick and wrapped head-to-toe in brightly-coloured fabrics, wait to greet someone important. One man is holding out a line of cigarette packages, trying to sell them by pack or by singles, ignoring how wilted they are by the humidity. Many are calling out or reaching out, but it is not a frantic scene. Most of them look a bit bored. But all are looking. Lena feels judged in that instant: pale, newly arrived, forged visa letter. They must see right through her.

Where is DJ? Could she be in a crowd like this? Blending in with a strong tan and relying on her Portuguese maternal tongue? Or has she gone off into the bush? Is she on her own, or has someone taken her? Lena shakes her head. No answers to the questions yet; this is only beginning.

'*Taxi? Queres taxi?*' Many voices at once crowd her ears;

17

unwanted hands jostle her elbows, making her pull her arms in closer to protect herself.

The other passengers are quickly sorted into greetings, car rides, package exchanges. They move beyond the barriers as if they have practised many times before. She looks back at the terminal building. Two Angolan officers sit behind the dirty glass doors that refuse to fully close. No return. She looks forward again and decides to go in the first taxi that looks like it might be safe. Good thing Lucien shared from his stash of US dollars. Hope they will do the trick.

'Are you…' A voice calls out more loudly than the others, with a clarity of direction aimed at her. 'You there, are you all right?'

She swings around to see a tall white middle-aged woman with a wide face, wearing a CWA t-shirt, the same organisation DJ works for. Lena laughs out loud with relief and moves towards the woman at the end of the rusty barrier. She is conscious of people watching her press through the line.

'Do you know DJ?' Lena jumps straight in.

The woman squints at her, deepening the wrinkles between her brows and at the corners of her eyes. She wears glasses with pink rims low down her nose, a beaded chain dropping down. Her hair is dyed bright red and tied in two plaits, like someone half her age. She doesn't smile. 'And you are…' she starts.

'I'm Lena, her sister. I've heard what happened, about the accident.' She can't afford to pause to let the woman contradict her and turn her away. 'I've come out to help.'

She feels the woman study her face a moment longer. Her assessment does not seem favourable. 'To… help?' she says.

She nods.

'Does Kojo know?' the woman asks.

She tries to remember the story she and Lucien worked on the night before she flew. It starts to fall apart in her head and she decides that observing more, saying less would be a better tactic. 'I talked to him a few days ago, but I'm not sure if he knows I'm here. Do you know where I can find him?'

'I'm heading to the office, after I pick up some freight that came on the flight.' A strong Irish accent comes through her phrasing. 'Want to wait? Or would you rather take a taxi?'

'I can wait.' She has a piece of paper where she's scrawled the address of the organisation's office she found on a website. Might not even be right.

'Okay, hang on a sec,' the woman says, and pushes back through the line of people towards the customs officers. Her flip-flops snap at heels that are dirty, calloused and cracked. Her broad shoulders hunch slightly as if she is anticipating a regular argument that she might just win.

'I'm Jeanette, by the way,' the woman says. 'Welcome to Malanje.'

They are in the car and she looks at Lena for a moment. Jeanette's mouth cinches tight as if there is more to say, but not yet. She turns away to start the ignition.

The car pulls onto the highway. Jeanette talks loudly above the engine noise,

'Have you been to Angola before?'

Lena shakes her head. 'Actually, this is my first time in Africa.'

Jeanette exhales. 'Hell of a place to begin,' she says. 'Has DJ told you much about Malanje?'

Again, she shakes her head.

'Well, it's not everybody's cup of tea, but you can grow to like it. It has some faded grandeur about it. There was a lot of money once upon a time, particularly with diamonds. Not now, though, with the war and the sanctions. Blood diamonds, they're called now, as if they're the things responsible for the bloodletting. Which, in a way, I guess they are. Anyhow, you are more likely to stumble upon a landmine than a diamond, nowadays.'

The road is crowded with cars spitting out diesel clouds. Bicycles and motorcycles are laden with people, sometimes whole families with children sandwiched between the adults. Chickens, goats and scraggy dogs are pushed to the margins but keep trying their luck for scraps near the traffic. A skinny cow crosses the road halfway, then startles and dashes back, to blasts of horns and shouts.

She has seen a photo, tucked into a letter some years back, of DJ standing sturdy next to a motorcycle. She wonders what it would feel like to ride here. How do you manoeuvre with so many people, vehicles and animals all over the road? How did DJ get to be so confident in this place?

Strips of low-lying shops advertise their wares with faded images of clothing, car parts, hair products. The colours are muted: pastels, browns, ochre, dirt-stained cement-grey. An official-looking government building rises up solid and concrete. It is scarred with pock-marks from what look like gunshots splayed in an arc across the façade. A church, slashed with a huge diagonal crack through the face, stands in defiance of any attack.

At a roundabout, a dozen men and boys hover on the periphery. Their clothes and faces have been sullied by the same grime and exhaust. They all are missing a limb, some missing two. Luckier ones have crutches or makeshift wheelchairs; others perch on the highway barrier. God knows how they manage.

Jeanette's car doesn't stop, barely slows as she zooms around the curve.

'Lena? Come in, come in.' She recognises the West African accent she heard before.

The director's office is a dark room lined with metal bookshelves displaying the faded spines of old publications. There is a wide desk stretching the width of the place. At the desk is a man with a round face, strong cheekbones, and smooth dark brown skin continuing up to a bald shiny head.

'Jeanette said she found you at the airport,' he says. 'We spoke on the phone. I am Kojo Appiah.'

She pauses in the doorway. She has been bracing for a fight and suddenly feels tired. She is no longer sure why she is here. But it would be awkward not to sit down, so she takes a seat in front of the broad desk.

'You have come out to Angola on your own initiative,' he says, not a question.

'Yeah, sorry. I was going to email you to tell you I was coming—'

He cuts her off. 'Even though I explained it was very dangerous.'

'I needed to come,' she says simply. 'She's my sister, I need to find her. That's what sisters do for each other, right? We're there for each other... and... the last time we saw each other...' Her voice trails off.

'I told you we would contact you as soon as there was news,' he says, in a tone that is less confrontational than she had expected. 'There is an ongoing police investigation into the accident, but it will take a while. We wanted to give DJ some time.'

He pauses, and she looks up and studies his face. She had expected at the very least obstructions, arguments stacked against her being there. But instead she sees something else. His eyes look worn out. They don't seem the eyes of someone who can hold onto anger for long. His expression starts to change in a subtle way as he returns her gaze.

She finds it too intense, and looks away. She wishes she was holding her camera, rather than having it sit wrapped up in her pack at her feet. Her hands twist in her lap.

'Well, you are here now,' he says.

'Can you tell me more about what happened?'

'It may be hard for you to hear. I know you two were close.'

She is about to disagree, but lets it go. 'How long has she been missing?'

'Ten days. As I told you on the phone, we had that terrible accident and one of our staff members, Maria, died. The neighbour radioed me, and we all came running. After the explosion, there was a fire and a lot of commotion. We did all we could to put out the fire, to try to save her and arrange a helicopter evacuation, but we… we failed.'

His voice falters for a moment, as he looks out of the window. 'With the war, you see, any unauthorised flight risks being shot at, possibly shot down. Flights need to get permission from both the MPLA authorities and UNITA, and still it is not clear if they will be safe after dark. I could not find a pilot willing to fly, even though I worked all the connections I have.

'I was so focused on trying to arrange the flight…' After another pause, he continues, his voice apologetic. 'And then when it all fell through, we looked up and realised that DJ had gone.'

'Gone, just like that?'

He nods.

'She didn't say anything?'

He frowns and shakes his head.

'On her own? What if something has happened to her?'

'We think it is possible DJ has gone off to see Maria's family, or is maybe trying to find out something about the accident. At this point we cannot be sure.'

'What if the explosion in the shack wasn't an accident?'

'We have been trying to think of who might want to do such a thing to Maria, but if you knew her, you would realise just as we have: she was universally loved. No one would have wanted to harm her.'

She looks straight into his face for a moment, giving him space to expand. There is more he isn't telling her, she can sense it. But that's fair; she hasn't earned it yet.

'So, as I said on the phone,' he continues, 'I do not think it's a good idea for you to be here.'

'I'm the only family DJ has,' she says quietly. 'Our parents died years ago.'

'But here, in a conflict posting, there are a lot of risks. You are not free to just wander alone. You would need logistical support.'

She looks down at the ground. She knows she didn't think it all through, didn't have access to the right information. But she still had to come.

'Can't I stay? Just for a short while? For DJ's sake?'

He twists his mouth left and right.

'I will give you a week,' he says.

Five

London, 1984

More than anything, even more than being a mother, Gloria felt she was born to be a midwife. It was not just a job, it was a call from God. Every Sunday, if she was lost for what to pray for, she gave thanks that she heard his calling. Even on days like this, when it had been a difficult shift, she knew she was pursuing her purpose.

Gloria felt the chair's angles as she sat down. Her body's softness was defeated by the drawn-out night shift. She wrapped both hands around the cup. It was cheap coffee, not how Eduardo made it. The cafeteria was cold at the seams, midwinter grey, London cold. The walls were a dirty wash of turquoise. The heating pipes above her head were losing insulation in peeling silver and fuzzy strips. That couldn't be good for your health. In Portugal, where she grew up, she didn't remember hospitals in the same state of disrepair. But maybe, as a teenager, she hadn't observed everything so closely.

She remembered watching the news of the Carnation Revolution in '74 on the black and white TV set in Eduardo's café in Stockwell. They were with all their friends, all immigrants from one place or another. She couldn't believe that the regime would fall, no one could. She remembered

24

holding Djanira, only four years old then, shushing her so they could hear the reports. But that girl, she was never able to keep still.

They shouldn't have chosen that name. *Stirring up great passion* – Eduardo's choice. She gave him his way with the name of their first born, a daughter who came from sin before wedlock. But they ensured the wedding vows were made before God, in time for her entry to the world.

DJ. Gloria worried about her. Fourteen years old and angry at everything. At her mother, at the state of the world, at who knows what. She wanted to only speak English. She cut her hair short like a boy. She was only happy when doing judo or fighting. Concessions brought just a temporary calm each time.

Lena was so very different. While DJ stormed ahead, Lena buried her face in her mother's skirt and went quiet. People sometimes thought she couldn't speak at all. But Gloria knew. Lena was an observer, saving judgements for later. Calm at the centre. Ready to help, but not leaping to conclusions. She'd make a good midwife, Gloria felt.

It was a grisly rain, the kind that made her blink too often, but not enough to stop and waste money on a new umbrella.

She never liked the neighbourhood much. The crowds, the loud roads. The Stockwell Green Estate was a maze governed by logic foreign to her. She felt repelled by the concrete ledges and stairways running everywhere, housing thousands of people. To her mind, the dark grey should have been hidden under plaster and paint in more dignified colours. Instead, it felt as if the neighbourhood wanted to expose its toughness, like showing off its tattoos and scars to anyone who walked by.

But Eduardo always looked on the bright side. 'At least they kept the buildings low,' he would say, almost convincing her.

'That way there's no one blocking out the sunshine for all the rest of us, eh?'

She was looking forward to seeing him. But she disliked the walk home, felt unsteady. Since the riots down in Brixton a few years ago, she wondered if it was a safe place for her girls.

What was DJ going to be stormy about today? Thoughts circulated in her head like flies that couldn't be swatted away: DJ was too much. She was too impulsive and explosive. She must get a handle on that temper of hers. Then her own guilty feelings swarmed in: it's my own fault for taking on so many night shifts at the hospital. I've been too tired. Haven't shown enough patience.

The air reeked of exhaust; even the rain couldn't rinse it clean. Too many lorries on these narrow roads. She had grown tired of turning her daughters away from the phone boxes decorated with postcards of prostitutes. Gutters constantly leaked rain, rubbish and mud from the overhead walkways.

She arrived at the café, and the bell dinged. A rush of warmth greeted her along with the smell of pastries. She managed a smile as she saw Eduardo in profile. He was such a handsome one, still. His face always a bit tanned, even in the winter. Anyone would think he was mulatto. The children, too, had his colouring, especially in the eyes. So dark you couldn't see the pupils.

The TV was showing a football match watched by a few regulars. Eduardo saw her and gave a wave. She sank into one of the padded yellow chairs by the window, looking out at the grey landscape.

'Where are the girls?' she asked.

'Outside, playing,' he called back, not taking his eyes off the set.

'Together?' She was surprised.

'Think so. With the Ramirez kids.'

Her mouth twitched.

He noticed, and came over with a cup of fresh coffee. The yellow padding made a 'shh' as he sat across from her. He leaned down and took hold of her foot. He slipped off the shoe, straightened her leg and started a foot rub.

'It's raining, they probably should come in,' she said.

'I'll go check, in a minute.'

Six

Kojo walks into the bar where he always finds Carlos on a Thursday. Something about the place cheers him up. They play soukous music, and occasionally some old school highlife, which makes him smile. The regular gambling night brings out all the men you'd expect to see – the local traders and businessmen and the police and the drivers from different organisations. Mainly Angolans, but a lot of others as well. There's the Mozambique clique, and quite a few Kenyans. The Moroccan medics, they keep more to themselves as they don't drink, but they do watch the gambling with a healthy interest. He's the only Ghanaian at the moment among the aid workers; others will probably rotate in and rotate out again.

Has he been in Angola too long? It's a question that has surfaced in his mind recently. Others advance in their career, going to work in different disasters and conflicts, joining the international management tier or the UN. But still he stays. He says it is because he is loyal to his team. He would not want to leave them in the lurch when it is such a difficult time. He is not the type of man to put his career above taking care of his people.

Also, he mastered the language, and that was not easy. He

has learned some Lingala and Kikongo too. He's proud of that. He loves the languages. He loves the shapes of the letters in his mouth. The soft way the Angolans have of making an S that sounds like a woman's hair on the pillow.

When he has had too much to drink, he admits to himself – and only to himself – that he fell in love with the language and the place because he fell in love with a woman. A woman can always change your view of where you are. She makes your senses come alive all at once, so that the new landscape, the work and the smells, including her scent, blend together. Your brain registers all this and tells you that you can be happy in a place, that this is where you should be.

Not that she loved him back. Their affair did not last many weeks, and was mainly in his mind. But he knows that was what held him here. Even after all these years, he does not have the urge to move on.

'Kojo, my man.' Carlos gives a wave from the bar and slaps the stool next to him. He is still wearing the MPLA uniform, having come straight from his work as head of police. 'What I want to know,' he says, as he pats a hand on Kojo's shoulder, 'is why you always seem so serious.'

Kojo manages a smile and indicates to the barman that he would like a beer.

'Maybe my friend here needs a woman,' Carlos continues. He doesn't look at Kojo to see if the words ring true. Carlos bends his head down to light a cigarette, then exhales out of the side of his mouth away from Kojo. He can be considerate like that, when he wants to be. 'Or maybe he has a wife hidden away, back in Accra who we never hear about?' At this, he looks up and tries to read Kojo's face.

It's a question he has had so many times before, stated or implicit. Most people assume that an African man of his age – they don't ask, but they can tell he is nearing forty – must have

29

a wife or wives somewhere. Some have one in every place they are stationed, children too. But Kojo, no. He could not do that.

Things would have been a lot easier if he had. He remembers the look on his mother's face when he refused to marry the Ashanti girl they had decided on. Not an arranged marriage, exactly, but one that would have been very convenient for both families involved. And she was beautiful, he could tell from the photograph. But kind? Or cruel? That you cannot tell from a picture.

And for some reason, his heart felt like a stone when he thought about marrying a woman he did not know. Who did not know him, on any deep level. He could see himself as if from above. He watched himself going through the decisions of the early courtship, choosing the kente cloth, hearing others plan the ceremony. He had this feeling of unreality taking over. It scared him, this separation of the thinking mind from the body doing the actions. The only way he could describe it was that it felt untrue. A lie, more profound than he had ever told before. Acting out a lie, in a way that would last forever. If he was not true to himself, then what meaning was there in anything? There would only be this lack of meaning, this un-truth, un-reality all around you and you couldn't live like that. He seriously worried that he would lose his mind if he followed through.

Many of his childhood friends were already married by then. He had to beg his father's forgiveness, knew that the insult would not be taken lightly in the extended family. He tried to explain to them this fear of living a lie, but they did not understand. Maybe they all did it? His brother, his father, they were all expected to come into line. Maybe they had some capacity he lacked; they could live with multiple versions of the truth, and he could not. Only his Auntie Oheama – who, it must be admitted, people thought was a bit mad and lonely herself – understood. Not completely, but enough to give him a way out. She recommended him to her cousin who was recruiting water engineers to work internationally.

And he has been abroad ever since. First in Lokichoggio, serving camps in South Sudan on the edge of that atrocious war. After three years in Loki he transferred to Luanda, then Malanje, managing all the operations and personnel.

In Malanje he met her, and it has rooted him to this position of director ever since. The fact that she did not love him, could not love him, has tainted the place, but still he has been there for years. Why? Habit? Desire? A sense of purpose? Who knows? Most days he is too exhausted from the work to examine it closely.

And now she is dead. So, did any of this matter? His feelings, his history? He is not sure, not any more.

'You still here with us, man?' Carlos runs a hand in front of Kojo's face to bring him back from his thoughts.

'Yes, sorry. I mean no. No wife. I tell you that all the time.'

Carlos smiles. 'You do. But I'm thinking that if I keep asking, I might get a different answer.'

'No, I am not that secretive, my friend.'

'Life might be more interesting if you were.'

'Perhaps, or maybe I'll leave that to you and the rest of the MPLA.'

Carlos gives him a close-lipped smile.

Seven

Jeanette's car pulls up into the gated drive of a villa painted yellow, faded with sunshine and heat. Bright purple begonias climb all over the door and gutters.

'That's Angelo, the night watchman,' Jeanette says, gesturing to a man with his feet on a chair in the shade of the outside veranda. 'Don't expect him to be awake any time soon. Don't expect much of him, actually.' There is a screen door that has been kicked in near the bottom. The wooden door behind is warped with age and heat.

Once inside, it's difficult to see. 'Sorry, except for the fridge for the vaccines, we only have electricity from six to eight pm, when we have a short shift with the generator,' Jeanette explains.

Lena's eyes begin to adjust. A staircase that might have once been grand spirals up to the next floor. Many steps are broken; it looks like a mouth with missing teeth.

Jeanette follows Lena's gaze. 'Mind the gap,' she says, mimicking a London accent.

In the next room sofas are covered with bright African prints in oranges, yellows and reds. At a table in a small kitchen in the corner, a white man frowns at his laptop. He is tall and curves over the screen in an uncomfortable hunch. He holds a cigarette between his lips while he jabs into the keyboard.

'Brad,' Jeanette says, 'this is DJ's sister. Her name's Lena.'

Brad looks up quickly, but his eyes dart back down to the screen to finish a task. Then he looks directly at her. She feels his eyes comb over her sweaty t-shirt, her hair falling out of her ponytail.

'Sister,' he repeats, taking the cigarette from his mouth. 'Didn't know you were on the arrivals list.' His voice has the flat metallic sound of the American south.

Her cheeks go red. Does he know about the fake letter? He looks confident, practical, well-informed. 'Kojo wasn't expecting me,' she manages to say.

Jeanette turns her back on them both and starts up a gas burner with a match. 'Cup of tea?' she offers.

Lena is grateful for the diversion and gladly accepts. She shifts the weight of her backpack onto the floor.

'Kojo gave her the front room for a week,' Jeanette says to Brad.

'Is that right?' His eyes stay pinned on hers longer than she wants, then he lets go. 'Welcome to our humble pad.' He goes back to the computer. 'These health stats don't add up,' he grumbles. 'Why does it list that we ran two clinics, when we ran a third one in Luremo? Didn't any kids get treated?'

Jeanette looks over his shoulder, rests a hand there for a moment. 'Have you added the UNICEF figures?'

He jerks away from her suggestion. 'Yeah, yeah, I thought of that, but they were inputted when they first came in.'

'What about last month's excess?'

'Just forget it. I'll figure it out.' He stands up abruptly, sweeps a few papers on top of the keyboard and snaps the laptop shut. 'See y'all later,' he says with little feeling. Taking the computer in one hand, he balances the ashtray in the other and moves with loud steps out of the room.

Jeanette watches the door for a moment, then turns to Lena. 'Would you like a shower? You must be sticky after your flight. Sorry we have no air conditioning, but the air does cool right down in the evening, you'll see. Feels good, except if you have malaria. You know what I mean?'

Lena's room is bare except for a bed with a mosquito net, and an empty shelf with an insecticide spray. There is a screened window, and she can sense the sleeping guard nearby. She is on the front side of the house, ground floor. It feels exposed.

So this is DJ's life, she thinks. The people she's close to, the job she was doing. DJ always liked life's rough edges.

As she goes upstairs, she skips over the broken steps and manages to get up using hands and feet together. In the bathroom, the toilet has a bucket next to it for flushing down. Another bucket, bigger, holds a jug with a bar of grey soap balancing on the rim. The tiles on the wall, broken away, testify to a working shower, some years back.

She strips down and pours the first jug of water over her head. The cold against her hot skin makes her gasp. Some water splashes in her mouth. Silly mistake, she scolds herself. She does not want to get sick out here and become even more of a liability.

She wants to be calloused already. She needs to prove something, but doesn't know what.

Eight

Jeanette and Brad take Lena to the Greek restaurant. It is a grand name for what proves to be a temporary shelter with tarps flapping across thin timber beams from a burnt-out roof. Inside, cigarette smoke is trapped and hovers just over the crowd. The place is filled with people, competing in the noise to be heard.

'This is it,' Kojo says, as he arrives to join them. 'This is where the great and the good come to mix.' He steers Lena and the others to a booth near the back. As she passes different conversations, she recognises Portuguese in the many tongues being spoken in the room, but it is decorated with different accents. The English, too, speaks from different origins: South Africa, Australia, India, others she can't place.

'What's to eat?' she asks.

'There's no menu,' Brad says. 'Four things are on offer: chicken, fries, orange Fanta, and Cobra beer. Sometimes there's no chicken. But today we might be in luck.'

'Doesn't sound very Greek,' she says.

'They just call it that because of the tablecloths,' Brad says, gesturing to the green checked plastic. 'And I think it used to be run by a Greek family, a long time ago. Before the war got so vicious in the eighties.'

'Don't really like this place,' says Jeanette, looking around. 'It's awful how everyone comes here to be seen.'

'Oh, it serves a purpose,' Kojo says, scanning the room over Lena's shoulder. 'It's useful to come out every now and then, to see who's visiting our corner of the world.'

Brad looks down and plays with a corner of the tablecloth. His fingernails are bitten down and his cuticles are peeling-scabbed. Jeanette shakes her shoulders as if trying to rid herself of nervousness, then turns to Lena.

'So you're a photographer – travelled much?'

She hates being the centre of attention. She tells them her old story about her interest in urban photography and landscapes, how London is the perfect place for endless exploration. She surely isn't convincing anyone at the table – they've made their living from going outside a narrow comfort zone. Kojo doesn't even seem to be listening. He keeps looking around the room, noticing every time the door opens.

'Does DJ come here often with you?' she asks.

Jeanette wrinkles her nose. 'Not into a lot of exposure,' she says.

'And such a good cook!' Brad added. 'Never needed this place. You're not a vegetarian, are you?'

She shakes her head.

He moves to get up. 'I'll order one for each of us, okay?'

She wishes she'd done more research before coming to Angola. There are so many things to ask, but she doesn't want to remind them of her lack of experience. Instead Jeanette and Kojo largely ignore her, as they talk about people she doesn't know and places she's never seen. She sits back and lets their conversation blend in with the rumble of other voices. African music dances over it all, tumbling from speakers above the bar.

The booth is small for the group of them and Kojo's leg presses against her own. Her jeans are too tight and constrained for this kind of heat. He's in khakis, seems much more in his element. She tries to examine his profile without being obvious. She likes the curve of his nose, how his cheekbones define the shape of his face. He has smile lines radiating from the corner of his eye. He would be fun to photograph. With a neutral background, using a macro lens. Smiling, relaxed.

But does he ever relax? He always seems to be working. He is talking now about the political situation. He says he is hoping to catch some people from Norway who might have the latest news about the ceasefire negotiations.

She wonders how long he's been here. Is he a typical UN kind of guy, jumping between situations and picking up women in each place? Does he have a girlfriend? Or a wife? She supposes these guys could have many flings if they wanted to. But he doesn't seem like that. There's a seriousness that has a hold on him.

Kojo moves to get up. 'Excuse me please,' he says. 'I see someone I recognise from the British Mission. It could be good to hear his take on things.' She slips her legs around to let him out of the booth. He approaches a table on the other side of the restaurant where three white men are sitting, and seems to be angling towards the tallest of them, the one wearing an expensive suit, minus the tie – the only person in here dressed that way. Is he trying to make a point? Then she remembers: he was on her flight from Luanda. The man in the safari hat, taking up too much space in departures.

Kojo stands, leaning slightly in to hear over the loud atmosphere. The man doesn't offer him a seat.

'I recognise that guy,' Jeanette says when Brad is back with four beers. 'Jacob somebody. From the FCO. The British Foreign Office,' she explains to Lena. 'Don't like him.'

'Why not?' Brad asks.

'Something about him. Can't remember. I think there was some conflict between him and Maria maybe, or...' She shakes her head and seems uneasy.

Just then, the suited man looks up and his eyes catch on Lena's for a moment. But he judges her uninteresting, and turns away.

'Anyway,' Jeanette continues, 'you can tell by his body language: crossed arms, leaning back, not really listening. All arrogance, coming up here for a few days at a time and telling us all how things are, totally divorced from the reality of what actually happens in these camps. Then he'll zoom back to London or wherever, suddenly the great authority on all things Angolan. Hate the type.'

'Kojo seems to respect his opinion,' Brad says.

'You know Kojo,' Jeanette says. 'He makes time for everybody and anybody. That's why he's so good at his job.'

Kojo comes back to the table when he sees that the chicken and chips have been served. 'So,' he turns to Lena. 'What are your first impressions of Malanje?'

She gestures that she is chewing and can't answer. In truth, she doesn't want to answer. It would sound stupid, whatever she came up with.

'The FCO guy is interesting,' he says to the others as he settles into his meal. 'Kept going on about how we need to be careful, with these rumours.'

'Rumours?' Jeanette says.

'The ones about the nurses poisoning people, remember?'

'I'm not worried,' Jeanette says, scooping up her chips a bit faster.

'I am not saying we should be worried,' Kojo says, 'but it is good to be aware of such things.'

'Do you take it seriously?' Lena asks.

'Well, if there are strong rumours, sometimes people may refuse to be seen as a patient in our clinics. If you have lost the confidence of the group, it can take a long time to regain that trust.'

She looks at him, expecting more.

'And then you can't work,' he explains, as if he assumed she would know the answer. 'You can't work without acceptance from the population. First lesson of humanitarianism.' He takes a long drink from his beer and seems to realise more explanation is needed. 'Our people are teams of nurses and water engineers, Lena. We just do health and wat-san. If people think there is wrong-doing, it could get difficult.'

'Or dangerous,' Brad adds.

'But we're not really paying attention to rumours,' Jeanette says quickly, sweeping up the bones to be discarded.

Nine

Kojo chews on his inner lip. His old friend starts to speak faster and louder, as she always does when she is upset.

'It's remarkable. She's nothing like DJ,' Jeanette says, back at the villa after Lena has gone off to bed.

He must admit she is right. Lena could contribute nothing of relevance. Nor did she show any understanding of what a drain she could be on the team. Another liability to juggle. It feels heavy, sometimes. A lot of the time.

He thinks back to how she was in the doorway of his office. Stood tall and sinewy as a new sapling. She shifted her weight from side to side, hips off balance. DJ used to stand in that same doorway, with her confident stance, square shoulders ready for confrontation.

'She's totally inexperienced, Kojo,' Jeanette continues, the volume increasing. 'What were you thinking?'

'I did not ask her to come,' Kojo says. 'She just came.'

'You could have said something to stop her.'

'I tried. She was determined.'

'How did she get a visa, anyways?' Brad asks.

'I don't know. Possibly she knows someone at the embassy? I was as surprised as you are.'

'And now we're stuck with her?' Jeanette continues. 'She is an awkward kid with nothing to offer.'

'It is true, she doesn't have the experience,' Kojo says.

'She's never been in Africa before! God Almighty.'

'I realise that,' Kojo says. He thinks back to Lena's olive skin, pale compared to the others here, not yet exposed to the sun. She seems delicate, but not altogether fragile. He feels a clash of emotions. Annoyance for the unplanned arrival, and something else: something about her is incomplete, and he senses that she could go the distance to fix it.

'Does she even have malaria tablets, or do I need to provide them?' Jeanette asks.

'I think she has all that.'

Jeanette blows air out through clenched teeth.

'Come on, Jeanette, it could be a good thing,' Kojo says. 'If Lena is here, DJ might come back to base.'

'But she doesn't know the first thing about DJ's life here.'

'I thought they were close, writing letters and such.'

'I'm not so sure.'

'Well you know, blood is strong. We offer DJ friendship, but there might still be too much anger.'

'Kojo, family relationships are complicated. Especially with someone like DJ.'

'You know DJ. Losing Maria, the tether to normal life is gone. Lena could be that reason to come back.'

She shuts the door to her room with a small click. She had run out of polite conversation, so made her excuses.

She couldn't say what she was really thinking. Why aren't they looking for DJ? Aren't they worried? She could be absolutely anywhere, alone and nowhere near home. What's wrong with these people? Why aren't they talking about it?

She knows enough to recognise that there is so much she does not know. She needs to understand the dynamics here, how people think and what compels them to act.

In her mind she rolls around the table like a camera on a 360-degree pivot. Jeanette, in profile: sharp nose, shapeless cheeks, talks a lot. Brad: no-fuss shaved hair, problem-solver. A thinker, but practical too. Kojo: sitting across, a bit gloomy. Lots of silences. As if he was composing something underneath the cover of conversation.

She could sense the tension in the group. Arriving uninvited was never going to win friends. But they weren't as obstructive as they could have been. She can get the ball rolling.

Changing into loose night clothes, she is relieved to lie down. Her body is worn out and her head fuzzy with tiredness.

There's a knock at the door. She sees Jeanette, holding a candle and a box of matches. 'You may want these if you're up in the night,' she says.

The door closed again with thanks, she sinks back onto the mattress. She shuts her eyes and feels again the circling of the plane coming in to land, over and over again.

She awakes disoriented. She is knotted in the sheets, sweating and anxious. Her mosquito net is askew. The clock says 2.08 am.

She wonders if the watchman is actually keeping watch. Is anyone out there at all, outside the front door? She wishes that she had something to hold for protection. She clings to her pillow with arms and legs wrapped around, as if it were a person. She struggles to get back to sleep with her head on the bare sheet, but she can't let go.

Ten

London, 1984

'Your sister is a freak!'

Lena's elbow hurt from how she fell to the ground. They had all been playing nicely on the roof of the multi-storey car park, near the hidden corner that was protected a bit from the rain. But now it all had changed. She felt the cold puddle-water seep through her jumper and her trousers. She willed herself not to cry. Six year-olds were not supposed to cry, especially not in front of older kids.

She looked up at Julia Ramirez's face and thought furiously what to say to get her to stop. She could feel the eyes of all the children looking.

'She's a freak. A lesbo. Don't you even know what that means?'

Lena didn't, but it couldn't be good.

'You'll be the same too if you don't watch out. It's catching.' Julia shook her hands like something was sticking to them. 'Better be careful!' Her blonde hair was held back by a pink headband, but some strands snuck out and stuck to the side of her face with the rain. Her mum let her wear blue eye shadow which usually made her look pretty and grown up, but now she looked angry and ugly.

43

Julia leered closer and held up her hand as if she might hit her. All Lena could do was curl up with her chin tucked in between her knees. She got colder and wetter on the ground. People would think she'd wet herself. It was not fair. Nothing about this was fair.

'You made her cry.' She heard Lucien's voice. 'That's not cool.'

'Well, she ought to know.'

'You wouldn't say that to DJ's face.'

Julia was slow to find a come-back. 'Course I would. I'm not afraid of DJ. She can't touch me.'

'Is that right?' DJ's voice was loud, bouncing off the wet angles of the car park.

Lena lifted her head from her protective ball. What would DJ do now?

Julia looked like she was struggling not to look scared. She was even uglier than before, her cheeks turning a blotchy pink-white.

DJ was in her judo stance – legs out sturdy like a warrior, hands ready, in fists. 'Who're you calling a freak?' she said.

Julia stepped away from Lena and rolled her shoulders back. She was older, but DJ was taller and was tougher, that was easy to see.

Lena got up quickly while Julia was distracted. She wiped her nose with her sleeve and hoped the kids would forget what happened. Her heart was beating too fast and she put her hands to her chest to try to calm it back down. Everyone knew that Julia picked on anyone who seemed scared. Today it happened to be Lena, tomorrow it would be Lucien, or somebody else, or her again.

The children were quiet for a moment. The rain could be heard bouncing off the concrete gutters.

DJ didn't look at Lena, eyes focused only on Julia. 'Jules, you're talking bollocks. You don't know shit.'

Lena covered her mouth to keep giggles in.

'What are you doing picking on little Mags, anyway?' DJ continued. 'She's done nothing to you.' DJ looked around now at the crowd of familiar kids. 'That's just cowardly behaviour, that.'

Julia's mouth twitched. Her arms were crossed in front of her chest.

'Nothing to say now? That's because you know bullies never win out.' DJ pressed her lips into a thin smile.

She looked around, and her eyes paused over Julia's bicycle. It was bright brand-new turquoise. There were silver and pink spoke-clickers in the wheels and a lovely basket perched on the handlebars; the loud bell made a *chi-ching* sound whenever Julia wanted to announce her arrival. They all knew it had been a birthday present, heard her bragging about it for weeks.

It wasn't locked.

DJ's eyes tightened into a sneaky look as she strode towards it. It wasn't small, but she lifted it up like a superhero, and held it high over her head. She spun around with it like that once, twice, to show how strong she was. Then she walked over to the edge of the car park, looked down for a second over the handrail, and threw it right over. Just like that.

Lena winced with the crash of metal and plastic and that bell-sound on the concrete two storeys below.

They all ran over to look. Lena saw the sad-looking thing clearly, still shiny new turquoise but twisted, like a horse that had broken its neck and would never get better. The back wheel was spinning, clickers flashing in the rain-grey light.

Shouts came up from below, some grown ups angry.

DJ didn't bother watching where it fell. She left them all

behind as she sprinted down the steps, triumphant, with her hands in the air like a championship fighter.

Eleven

Gloria looked out from her favourite vantage point in sight of the bridge, near the sheltered corner where she had first kissed Eduardo. The summer evening was coming in, the hot air of the city being pushed away by cooler sea-scented winds. The breeze brought a tingle to the surface of her skin, and she couldn't help smiling at the thought of seeing him again.

The river Tejo washed below, wide and grey-blue, reaching out to the ocean two kilometres away. Where does it go, the water? Out to the Azores, Capo Verde and beyond? To the Colônias. She had heard about life there. Sounded like a fantasy – living it up like a rich person in a country of poorer people. White men acting like kings in a way that they never could in Lisbon. She knew some boys who had their minds set on that experience. They said they would find diamonds, and never have to work hard again.

But that wasn't her kind of adventure. She was destined for London. Knew it for the longest time, since she first started volunteering at the Hospital de Santa Maria. Working with the sisters, it didn't matter whether she was changing bed-pans or giving medicine to some sweet old grandmother who had no one. She knew. God had signalled to her heart and showed her the calling.

London, with the recruitment programme for nurses, would be the perfect escape. A city of lights and music and dancing and living freely with other girls. She couldn't wait.

But then came Eduardo. Tall man, long limbs and big hands. His island skin was dark and leathered by the salt. A handsome, kind face. When he was dressed up in white pinstripes, he had a glimmer of perspiration in the heat. He didn't seem made for a suit. He stood out from the others – he seemed to totally lack their aggression. They were merely boys, smoking and posturing like peacocks. Overcompensating for their lack of experience about what manhood entailed. None of them had yet been out in the world. Eduardo had a steadiness about him that skimmed over all of that like a catamaran on choppy waters.

Gloria's friends clustered together like bees protecting the queen. Her eldest sister Eugenia played the starring role. Euridice, the second-born, was the lady in waiting. Their skirts pirouetted as they twisted and turned, trying to show themselves from what they hoped were all the best angles. They were doing their best to look like models from a fashion magazine, but pretending at all times it was a lucky accident.

The boys huddled nearby, keeping up the pretence of not being bothered. As the evening progressed, the two crowds would start to mingle as they always did. Everyone was trying to give the impression that no one cared about the outcome. But they had nothing else in their heads at all.

It never changed, this dance of the sexes. Everyone watching out of the corner of their eyes. The same people, having the same conversations. Sooner or later they would pair up and marry in a grand wedding at the cathedral and then the fuss would be over.

None of them would last a day in London. It was as if they had heard the songs of Marianne Faithfull or the Rolling Stones, could pretend to like them, but they couldn't admit that the ideas themselves were too foreign. The meanings were impenetrable for narrow-minded people like them.

As the groups began to blend in the falling light, after the river had swallowed the last of the sunset, he had found her. He introduced himself and told her he was visiting a cousin for the summer. He talked about his home in Funchal and the islands, his sisters, his father's bakery. She found herself smiling and shy, grateful for the yellow-green streetlamps that might hide her blush. She wasn't usually like this. Her sisters always said she was too outspoken and impulsive, but this man made her feel different. She wondered how long he was here for, and if she could convince him to stay longer.

He came again the next night. And the one after that. Each time they both observed the movements of the others as if they had been scripted. Then they met in the margins.

She started to feel less reserved. She told him her opinions about the others, and her blunt views made him laugh. She talked about her plans to study nursing, how she was going to be the first woman in her family to get a degree and get out of Portugal.

How did they end up alone on the sandy riverbank under the bridge? She barely knew him, this strong and confident man. Unlike Father, he didn't smell of fish and old socks. He smelled delicious – like cinnamon, almonds and the sugar-syrup that surrounded *fios de ovos*. He spoke about the bakery he wanted to open, and hinted that he wanted her there with him.

She was conscious of his arm, which had been loosely at her waist, pulling her closer.

He leaned in close to her. 'May I ask you a question?'

'Why not?'

'A personal question?'

She nodded.

'May I kiss you?'

She giggled and could not say the words.

His eyes opened wider, like a child presented with unexpected sweets. 'Is that a yes?'

She moved to kiss him, not really sure how. She had seen it in *Casablanca* and a few other films at the cinema, but Father Alfredo had ensured that most of the kissing parts were cut out before the films were shown to the crowds.

But she wasn't thinking of Father Alfredo for long.

She was amazed by the fizzy feeling of Eduardo's tongue on her tongue, his soft lips knowing exactly what to do.

She stopped him when she thought the others would notice how long they had been gone. Out of breath, she tried to pull her thoughts back from the whirlwind of kisses and caresses which had untucked her shirt, undone her buttons and put her hair all in a mess.

His eyes crinkled at the corners and she could tell he was pleased. His hair also needed to be smoothed.

'We need to pull ourselves together,' she said.

'So sorry, *minha querida*, you've lost a button.'

She wished he hadn't seen. 'I'll have to hide it somehow.'

'I'll buy you a new one tomorrow. Take my jacket?'

She pulled it over her shoulders, loving the scent of him that came from the collar. But Eugenia would know. Euridice too. They would let something slip awkwardly in front of Mother. They would never understand how she wanted to step out of the choreography.

She suppressed a smile all day, waiting for the evening. They always found a way to meet under the bridge. But she couldn't tell anyone. If they found out... Father, he'd turn against her. Mother would only repeat her refrain about wild women bringing shame to the family. Her sisters were amused and puzzled at her bursts of good humour and temper, not knowing the cause. Couldn't they see how tight and old-fashioned their lives were, now that she had found someone entirely different?

Eduardo went further. The first time he reached under her skirt, she was shocked and pushed him away.

He jumped back, as if suddenly awakened from a dream.

'Sorry, *minha querida*,' he said softly. 'Don't be angry. Come back, come here.'

She felt a wash of upset feelings all in a mix. She looked down, smoothing out her clothes. This had got out of hand. She needed to get her head straight.

'Gloria, for the love of God, look at me.' He had her lipstick smudged around his mouth, but still managed to look handsome. His black hair fell into his eyes and he attempted to coax it back into place. His face was not quite able to stifle a smile, even though he was trying to look serious. 'I think I've fallen in love with you.'

'You can't,' she said. 'We've only known each other a few days.'

'I can. You try to stop me.' He moved closer to her. 'Here, I'll keep my arms above the waist, is that all right?' His arms opened, like a bear inviting her home to his cave. She let herself be enveloped by his warmth. She smelled his sweat and marvelled at how she even liked that, too.

He kissed the top of her head. 'You awaken great passion

51

in me, like a Djanira, you know? I've never known another woman like you.'

'I'm going to London,' she reminded him. 'In just three weeks. You'll meet another woman soon and forget me.'

'Never. You'll have to take me with you.'

She pulled back and looked at him. 'You, in London? You hate cities! You spend all your time talking about wanting to get back to the peace of the islands as soon as possible!'

'That was before.'

'Before…?'

'This,' he said, and kissed her again on the lips as if making a promise.

After a moment, he paused. 'I forgot, I have something for you.' He reached into his pocket and pulled out a small velvet bag tied with a ribbon. He handed it to her and stepped back a little. 'Open it,' he said.

She took the smooth package and undid the bow, shaking it a little. A necklace tumbled into her palm. She looked up at him, not understanding.

'It's St Christopher,' he said. 'Don't you know?'

She shook her head. In the palm of her hand lay a delicate chain, with a medal the size of a small coin. In the fading light under the bridge, it was hard to make out the embossed design.

'He's for travellers. The saint who protects people who are going to travel. It's to keep you safe even when you are far away in London.'

No one outside of her family had ever given her a gift like this before. She didn't know what to say.

He asked if he could fasten it around her neck. Once it was there, she put her hand over the medallion as it rested above her breastbone. It wasn't heavy, but wearing it made her feel different. She felt like a woman, tied to one man.

She hadn't been planning to do it. She was going to stop him, like last time. But when it came down to it, and he spread his jacket out on the sand under the bridge, she had to admit to herself that she wanted to.

She wanted to see what it felt like, to be with a man. This man.

His touch was smooth and exciting. She loved his hands. On her breasts, she felt this energy that went up around her shoulders, neck, mouth, and down past her stomach. He reached under her skirts and this time she didn't stop him. She gasped at the feeling as he ran his hand on her skin just on the inside of her underwear. She shut her eyes. She didn't want to see this. She wanted to feel it.

He pressed his hips against hers and she felt his firmness. She didn't know what would happen next, what should happen next.

His hand went first. She twisted her head left and right in the sand, finding it incredible to have such an escalation of feeling with these tiny movements between her legs. He tickled the outside, playing softly with the hair. She laughed and then covered her mouth with a hand. Surely you were not supposed to laugh, right?

One finger played with her, gently and then more insistent. Two fingers. Then pressing deeper. She felt such physical pleasure she wanted to cry out, but also… would it hurt? The girls, the ones with married sisters, they said it hurts the first time. Made you bleed. God's punishment for our womanly sins. Oh, is this what sin feels like?

She heard him shift his weight and unzip his trousers. This is it, she thought. She lay flat, trying not to disturb him.

'I love you,' he said again. He didn't seem to expect a reply.

Then he pressed into her. Slow at the entry, then with a jerk that made her gasp in pain.

Oh, it was too much, this thing inside her. But it was too late now. She turned her head away.

He held his weight with one arm in the sand, the other one on her hips to guide the motion. He started coming in and out. Actually, the pain was gone, something had broken and let him inside deeper. He was still there, and the feeling, while not quite as nice as the caresses before, was interesting. Feeling smooth and wet. She was curious but also a bit ashamed.

He increased his rhythm as he came in and out of her, and she liked the sensation. But nice girls weren't supposed to enjoy this kind of thing, not with boys from Funchal they barely knew. And yet she did.

Who has to know? Maybe no one. Not the girls. Not Father Alfredo. And God? Well, if God watches everything, then he knows already.

Eduardo moved back and forth, his breath getting raspy and rapid. 'Oh Lord,' he said, like a man afraid. He grunted a long noise and arched up his back, as if driving his pleasure into her one last time. Then he stopped.

She opened her eyes a little. He moved to the side, the flaps of his shirt hiding him from her view. His legs, long and hairy, looked comical without the trousers.

'Are you okay?' he asked.

She rolled to face away, pulling her skirt down to cover herself and reached for her panties. She touched down there and brought up her hands. Her fingers were red with blood.

'Did it hurt? Was it your first time?'

'Of course it was.' Too many questions. What kind of girl did he think she was? 'Can I have that?' She reached for his handkerchief, tucked in the pocket of his suit jacket on the ground.

'Sure, anything.'

Turning her back to him, she arranged it as a pad to catch the drops. She had bled into the fabric of her skirt too. Going to be difficult to hide this from the girls, but she'd find a way somehow.

'You've changed me too, you know,' he said.

She gave him a disapproving look. She knew the consequences from the deed are borne by women, not men.

'No.' He saw her scepticism. 'You have. You don't see it, but you have.'

'How so?'

'Love. It reinvents us. I used to be a baker from Funchal. Now you've turned me into a man hopelessly in love with a woman going to London.'

She half-smiled at him. Hopeless? Why was he hopeless? Didn't she just give him something to be happy about?

'I'll come with you,' he said. It was a suggestion. From the look on his face, one that he was praying she'd take up. 'Shall I?'

Twelve

The wind is bitter on your cheeks, as the landscape blurs in your peripheral vision.

You know the way. You focus your concentration on the surface coming under your front wheel. Tree roots, potholes, anything could knock the bike off-course. Newly laid dirt could signal hidden landmines. You know that you can't drop your concentration for a second.

The trees create a canopy over the road, which follows the river bed. They provide respite from the afternoon heat.

You have ridden this way so many times, but never alone. Even as your arms remain strong and braced against the handlebars, the pain in your chest makes you want to cave inwards and give up. Always in the past you have had her arms around your waist.

It's her community which welcomed you. Those times when others shunned you. Threatened you, jeered. Her group of gentle believers let you both in, refrained from questions, gave you sanctuary.

You can't picture anywhere else now. You might cease to exist if you don't make it there, and soon.

The top layer of your skin screams as if it is about to wrench free, but still you urge the motorcycle forward.

Thirteen

The car approaches a group of soldiers in grey-green fatigues gathered on either side of the road. There is a chain slung between two mounds. All the men have machine guns strapped over their shoulders. One man is leaning on his like a walking stick.

'That's strange,' Kojo says. 'New checkpoint.'

As the car gets closer, Lena is surprised to see how small the boys look, barely teenagers, if that. The youngest boys seem tasked to hold the chain taut. It would be a laughable threat, except that one of them is pointing his gun directly at Sebastião, the CWA driver. Next to this gunman is a taller man, with a stony, still face. His eyes remain hidden behind large sunglasses.

'Don't say anything,' says Kojo in a low voice. The car stops a respectful distance from the boys. The tall man approaches the car and demands to see papers. Their passports are passed through Sebastião's window to him.

He is young too, she thinks. Younger than me, although his uniform looks like it's been through a few battles.

The soldier's machine gun rests on a strap just below his

58

elbow, his hands free to linger on the pages. He flips through each passport slowly.

'Ghana.' The solder looks at Kojo.

'*Sim Senhor.*'

'*Britânico.*' The soldier moves his sunglasses down to look at Lena. She is startled to see how bloodshot his eyes are. She doesn't know whether to smile or stay still. She chooses a tentative smile.

'*Sim*, that's me,' she says.

He pauses, holds her passport up longer than Kojo's. She looks straight ahead and wonders if she's failing her first test.

The soldier holds onto the passports as he moves to look under the car. From behind he bangs on the boot of the car to demand that they open up.

'Stay calm,' says Kojo.

Sebastião speaks quietly and smoothly to the soldier through the window in a string of words mixing Portuguese with another language. He lifts his hands from the wheel, and making large and slow gestures, takes off his seatbelt and shows his intention to open the door. The soldier's expression does not change to stop him. He climbs out of the car slowly, as if nothing could bother him. The car door swings back behind him, not quite shut. The keys are in place and the engine is gently running.

Sebastião walks to the back of the Land Rover, speaking in low tones. The soldier jabs towards the boot with his gun, the other hand still holding the passports. Sebastião keeps talking, the musical tones coming into the car muffled. He slowly opens the back of the vehicle, saying, '*Medicamentos, tratamento de aguas...*'

The soldier leans slightly forward, then after a moment steps back. With a nod, he allows Sebastião to shut the boot again.

Sebastião stays next to him a bit longer, exchanging a few more words, offers him a cigarette. The solder takes the whole pack. Then he tosses the passports back through the car window as he walks back to his companions.

Sebastião climbs into the car, belts up, and shifts into gear. The soldier jerks his chin to nod to the younger ones who drop the chain to the ground. The car crunches over the barrier in the red dust, and they are through.

Lena lets downs her clenched shoulders. Her pulse throbs in her throat. Breathe, she says to herself. Toughen up. She looks at Kojo in the front seat. Don't let them see how nervous you are.

'This could be distressing. Are you sure you want to see it?' Kojo asks as the car pulls into a drive.

'I think it's necessary, don't you?' Lena replies.

'If you say so.'

Sebastião turns off the engine and looks at his boss. '*Tem cuidado chefe,*' he says.

'*Sim, Sim,*' Kojo says, patting Sebastião on the shoulder. 'We'll be careful.'

She moves to open her door, but Kojo stops her. 'Take your time. There was the explosion. And there might be mines here too, new ones. We'll only walk where we can see tracks already down. You need to walk literally in my footsteps, okay?'

She nods, and lets him get out of the car first before slipping out of her door. Her camera bangs against her hip as she slides the strap on.

'We never stray from the path,' he says. 'You have to appreciate the prevalence of landmines here. We always need to be vigilant, use all of our senses, and look twice.'

The driveway curves towards a rusted yellow gate with a

padlock and police tape. 'They sealed the place off,' he explains. 'They say there is to be a thorough investigation. But I don't think that would happen unless we started bribing a lot of people. Unfortunately, that's not how we do things.'

He looks around and then climbs over the fence. He gestures for her to do the same. 'Do you need a hand up?'

'No thank you.' She swings her legs over then hops down. In front of her the red earth is streaked with black ashes, ground in by tyres and footprints that came before. The morning light is gentle, filtered through the trees. She brings her camera up to her eye.

'Observe it first,' he says, 'and then decide if it is something you want to preserve in pictures.'

She lets the camera swing back over to her side.

The dry earth crunches underfoot. A harsh burnt smell surrounds them as they move towards a black hulk. Scorched timber lies fallen, leaning on itself like an altar with all the angles wrong. Her eyes make out how there could have been a cabin, the shape is square and large enough. But the structure has lost all integrity and colour. Black and grey have taken over, and their domination is nearly complete.

She runs her hand down a vertical beam of what might have been a doorway. The burnt wood is smooth and silvery, like the ash was first painted on, then absorbed, transforming the texture. She tries to imagine what it was like when it was whole and inhabited. Scenes of fire flash up in her mind and she can't shake off the idea of the explosion targeting her sister.

'This was their front veranda,' he says. 'We spent many an evening here, finishing up donor reports or having a drink.'

She tries to imagine the team there, together, before the accident. 'DJ does like a drink,' she says.

He looks at her, surprised. 'Yes, that's true. But it never

makes her lose control. That is the thing about DJ, quite disciplined, in her own way.'

'Is she? That's not how I remember her.'

'No? Well, I suppose people can change. With time and distance.'

She nods, although she doesn't completely agree. 'Tell me more about that night.'

'There's not much I can tell,' he says. 'DJ and Maria had dinner with us. They didn't seem worried about anything. It was an ordinary day's work at Quessa camp, where we run a regular clinic. They came back here and apparently the electricity was out. There was a gas leak they didn't sense, and Maria lit a match.'

She shudders, looking at the destroyed cabin ahead of her. 'It could've happened to anyone, then?'

'I suppose so.'

'Are you sure?'

He frowns.

'Is there anyone who would have had it in for my sister? Or Maria?'

He chooses his words carefully. 'Everyone loved Maria. You should have seen her, the way she was with people. I've never known a better nurse.'

'And DJ?'

'You think someone wanted to hurt DJ?'

'It's possible, isn't it?'

He looks at the burnt shack in silence.

She can hear him breathing, and the wind in the trees. A large vehicle rumbles by on the road below, out of view.

'Can we go inside?' she asks.

'Better not. It could collapse.'

'Shame,' she says, leaning closer to look. Different layers of surfaces jut out at all angles. Some are ruined by fire or water.

Others maintain a veneer of normality. A patch of blue paint is visible, and a snatch of some wording. The corner of a poster? Or a notice of some kind? She brings her camera to her face and starts to take photographs. She is glad she loaded it with black and white, best for contrast. There is little noise except for the blink of her shutter as he watches her work. She steps back to go to the other side of the shack.

He follows her. 'Stay on the concrete foundation, if you please,' he says. 'They lay booby traps in the tall grass.' He points to the right. 'That way people can't get away when the soldiers come to take the boys and men for the army.' He pauses, then adds, 'Or the women.'

Not taking her eye away from the viewfinder, she asks, 'What do they do to the women?'

'You don't want to know.'

She keeps clicking the shutter, catching the different angles.

'Are you sure you will want to look at these pictures again?' he asks.

'This is how I remember a place,' she explains. 'Makes it into something I can decipher later.'

'I can't see that there's anything worth saving,' he says.

Nothing left. She puts her camera down when the roll is finished.

Turning back to him, she asks, 'Why do you say that there may be booby traps set, if you're convinced it was an accident?'

'There could be traps or mines anywhere. We found some just there, beyond the back door. There's no logic, sometimes.'

She watches the wind move the tops of innocent-looking grass, trying to imagine a world with no logic.

'Can I see where they spent that last day?' she asks. 'Was it Quessa camp you said?'

'What for?'

'To talk to some people? Maybe learn more about her life

here. Might give me a clue as to where she's gone. Time's ticking on, you see...'

'We have a visit this afternoon, but I had not planned on taking you along.' He looks at her directly. 'If you come to Quessa, can we trust you? This isn't a holiday, you know. It is dangerous out here, and I need to know that you will follow the protocols.'

She pulls herself up a bit taller. 'Understood. I won't do anything stupid.'

He tries to read her face for a moment, then seems satisfied. 'Come on, let's go back and get the others,' he says.

She pivots and looks at their trail, neatly printed with the larger treads protecting the smaller ones.

Fourteen

Lena is in the passenger seat bouncing over a red dirt road, riding next to Sebastião. He emits a sense of calm despite the fact that he is always in motion to respond to bumps, potholes, animals or people in the road.

She examines his hands. Large hands, like her father's were. Strong grip. She puts her trust in him. But the others, she's finding them harder to understand. Why aren't they worried about DJ? The team of people, Kojo in particular, seem to be too calm, almost suspended above the reality of this place. Don't they realise that the more days that go by, the harder it will be to find her? Where is their sense of urgency?

Or maybe they are still in shock about the death of Maria. But this is a war zone. Shouldn't they be used to death by now?

But she can't say any of that. She needs to build up the picture of what is going on here, and how these people interact. Maybe if she understands the context better she'll see some detail that the others have missed.

'Does DJ usually come in the Land Rover with you?' she asks.

'She always drives out on her own, on the bike,' Kojo says.

'And you are okay with that? Safety protocols and everything?'

She can see in the visor-mirror that, behind her, his eyes show a hint of a smile.

'We usually move in convoy, that's true,' he says. 'There is better safety in numbers. But DJ needs to be on her own sometimes. She probably knows the roads better than me.'

She looks through the windscreen streaked with red dust. The road twists and curves, with little to differentiate one mile from the next. How do you possibly get to know a road like this?

The wing mirrors reflect arcs of mud streaking from the tyres as the car negotiates the obstacles. 'How long has the conflict been going on?' she asks.

'It's been twenty-six years of this,' he replies. 'Lately there have been more guerrilla tactics – seizing food from houses, kidnapping children, and attacking unguarded villages at night. We need to be especially careful about security when we travel, and after dark. There is a feeling like we could be heading towards some kind of brink.' He pauses, but then continues, faster: 'But we are just engineers and nurses, not political analysts. We don't really know what's going to happen.' He turns to Jeanette. 'What do you think?'

Jeanette sits up with a jolt as if she had been daydreaming out of the window. 'What's that? I don't know the politics. I only know that this war is brutal and people are tired. Bloody tired. Some people are newly displaced, others have been displaced again and again. They don't want this.' She gestures out towards the landscape, as the car turns left and it becomes clear they are approaching a settlement. 'They didn't ask for this. They have no choice.'

The car slows as potholes and ridges grow more frequent.

Lena's fingers move nervously over the zipper on her camera

backpack. She no longer knows if this was a good idea. How much can you learn about a person in their absence?

Around a small bend after a mound, a big blue-and-white UN sign announces Quessa camp. Behind it, dark grey canvas tents come into view. The tents collect in curving, imperfect lines that follow the landscape of dry hills. There are thousands of them, impossible to count.

'How many are there?' she asks.

'About 35,000 people at this camp,' says Kojo. 'We have worked here for three years, and the numbers swell at key moments in the fighting. Recently there are new arrivals in bad shape. Jeanette is running a clinic, the one Maria ran last time.'

The clinic is a bare wooden shack painted white, stained with the red dust. A line of women, children and old men squat around the doorway. Their eyes look up at the CWA team. If they are surprised, they only show a mild interest and they don't move from where they are.

'Many of them have malaria,' Jeanette says. 'I can see how tired they are. Tired in their bones and their faces. I know how that feels.' She takes a long breath. 'Although there are a lot of nutrition cases here too. Let's see what we can do.'

'The team has a lot going on today,' Kojo says to Lena. 'If you wait near the clinic I'll find someone who worked with DJ the last time we were here.' He starts to get out of the car, but then leans back in. 'However, you must keep in mind that people are very busy, so they may not have a lot of time for your questions.

'And if you want to take photographs,' he continues, 'that's generally fine, but remember what I said about acceptance? You need to ask permission to take someone's photograph, with words or with gestures. If they shake their head no or turn away, then that is that. You do not press it, okay? They have already been through more than you can imagine.'

She nods, and tries to get out of the car without drawing attention to herself. She watches Kojo talk for a few minutes in rapid Portuguese to the local team members about the work. She lets her eyes rest on his face as he talks. She wonders what DJ thought of him. Did they work well together, or did they clash?

She squints as she takes in the landscape and thinks about how to photograph it. The sky is unforgiving, with just wisps of clouds in thin horizontal strokes. The tents are more-or-less identical cones, each the same uniform grey over the sandy ground. Everything feels stunted and hot. The dust at ground level is contradicted by the exuberant blue of the sky. The mid-morning sun could put people's faces in too much contrast to make a good picture. Best to use the UV filter and make the most of the shade.

Kojo approaches her, bringing a local colleague. 'Andreas is one of our best engineers. He worked with DJ the last time she was here,' he says. 'DJ is the team leader of the water engineers. They work on distribution networks and bladders.' Reading the blank expression on her face, he adds, 'It's just a basic system of sanitation, to provide water to clinics and public gathering points.'

'You know DJ well?' she asks Andreas.

He nods and looks at Kojo.

'How's your Portuguese, Lena?' Kojo asks.

'A bit rusty, haven't spoken it much since my mum died, but I can understand.'

'He'll show you around then.'

Andreas has a kind face, she judges, and she is grateful when he leads her towards a path between the tents. He talks in a steady stream of Portuguese interspersed with another language she does not recognise, but that could also be technical jargon.

He shows her a line of newly built latrines in bold blue plastic for her to photograph. In a different direction, he traces pipes installed from a large truck-mounted water tank to a pair of taps standing sturdy up out of the ground. '*Agua potável*,' he says with pride.

Women and girls huddle around the taps, jugs of various shapes and sizes at their feet, on their hips, or on their heads, as they each wait their turn. An older woman pulls and fusses over the hair of a younger woman squatting at her feet. Lena wants to approach the women, but she can't think of a way to do it and not feel so out of place. One girl sets herself apart, maintaining her spot in the queue but her back to the others. Her torn wrap is faded with wear and sun. She stares into the distance like someone with memories she wished were never hers.

Andreas leads Lena to a large concrete water table. It is rectangular and flat, with space for a dozen people to wash clothes. A woman stands at an angle facing away from Lena, scrubbing hard at some garments. She has a baby tied on her back who jiggles with the rhythm. The woman's sleeves are torn off at the shoulder, and Lena can see the muscle fibres taut and shifting under the skin.

Two other women are washing laundry at the table, but they stop when they see Lena. She gives an awkward wave, which they do not return.

'*Bom dia, senhoras*,' she says.

They stare at her.

Andreas smiles and speaks a cascade of words that she does not understand, in friendly tones. The women do not smile, eyes lingering on her. Not just on her face, but on her body, clothes, shoes and camera. Eventually they go back to their washing.

'You and DJ, you did all this?' she asks in Portuguese.

Andreas nods, and adds a long list of names of other people who worked together on the project.

'What is DJ like, when she is working?' she asks.

Andreas looks at her with a puzzled expression.

'Does she focus down on a task, or does she stand up, like a director, and tell people what to do?'

He repeats that they worked together on the latrines, the washing table and the drinking taps. He seems disappointed that she fails to appreciate these successes.

She asks if Andreas ever heard DJ talking about going away somewhere. He frowns and shakes his head. She presses him further, asking if there was anyone who was angry at DJ or had any reason to hold something against her. To each question he goes on at length and speed to assure her that DJ was well liked and respected for her work. '*Ninguém toca nele*,' he says.

Eventually she thanks him for his time and lets him go back to the work he needs to do.

'"No one would touch DJ,"' she reports back to Kojo, when she finds him again near the clinic. He is examining some water piping problem in the ground. 'That's what he said.'

'Is that so?' he asks, looking not at her but down at a tangle of grey plastic pipes emerging through mud.

'Said a lot of things. Really interesting. Great work here, by the way.'

He still doesn't look up to acknowledge her.

'Just one thing,' she adds. 'Why does he keep talking about DJ as *ele*, a he, not *ela*? Is that a dialect thing? I kept getting confused.'

He glances up for a moment until a squelch of mud draws his gaze back earthward. 'It's a cultural thing,' he says. 'Machismo is very strong here. They refer to the team as a group of men, and the leader as a man. Like soldiers to a captain. You could fight it, or go with it. DJ went along with it.'

*

Lena sits in the shade of the late afternoon, waiting for Jeanette and the others to finish their work so they can get on the road before sunset. She feels frustration building up in her. From other people pushing her concerns aside, setting her back.

She goes off to find Kojo. 'Are you almost finished with your work?'

'It's never finished,' he says. 'That is what keeps us humanitarians going.'

'Could you come with me to ask a few questions, if you don't mind?'

He pauses, reluctant.

'Maybe someone else who knew DJ? Saw her working here last time?'

'All right. Let me wash this mud off my hands.'

He brings her into a new section of the camp. 'Stay here a moment,' he says, as he darts down a narrow side path.

She feels hot, dusty and dirty. Nothing accomplished for the day. What was she doing here? How was she going to find DJ if all she did was wait around?

She reaches her hand towards a woman walking by. She doesn't mean to grab her arm, means only to touch it in a tentative way, but somehow her hand becomes wrapped around it.

The woman stops abruptly. She is holding the hands of two children and they too turn and look startled at this white stranger who has stopped their momentum.

Lena's breath won't let her speak as she loses the words she planned to say. She looks directly into the woman's face and sees intensely green eyes. She has never seen that colour iris with dark brown skin.

She wants to release the woman's slim arm but knows she

must say something. '*Desculpa*, sorry,' she says, her voice trembling. Mixing languages, she stumbles. '*Minha irmã*,' she manages. '*Estou procurando,* my sister. She has gone missing.'

'*Sua irmã*,' the woman says back, her lips drawing out the S sound in a way that seems to calm the sentence, soothe Lena's nerves. The children stay connected to their mother, shifting from one foot back to the other. One child is a tall boy, nearly a teenager. Loyal and protective, he moves closer to her. There is a girl as well, and a baby tied to the mother's back with colourful but fading cloths.

Lena tries to find words to describe DJ: '*Ela é alta, forte, trabalhou como engenheira…*' Her voice trails off. How do you paint a picture of someone they have clearly never met?

The green eyes blink slowly. No recognition.

Kojo comes running towards the women. He takes Lena's hand off the woman's arm, looking at her like she is out of control. '*Desculpa, desculpa…*' he says to the woman. He explains in Portuguese that Lena is a stranger visiting here, upset by her sister going missing.

She steps back, chastised.

She watches him as he talks to the woman. She wishes she could be smooth with strangers like him. That new situations didn't turn jarring and awkward.

The woman, now that her walking was interrupted, seems mildly interested. She speaks Portuguese and introduces herself as Fernanda. She didn't know DJ, but in agreeing to stop to speak to them, she wants something in return. She explains how she and her three children fled their town when UNITA came looking for child recruits. Then the rebels kidnapped Fernanda's pregnant sister, Kudielela, instead. Nothing has been heard of her since. Fernanda prays every day they will find her and that the baby was born safe and unharmed.

72

Lena watches the woman speak. She has sharp cheekbones, with graceful lines running around her mouth. She is quiet and measured in her language, yet her sentences come out with a melody that shows she has not given up. Lena is envious of the kind of strength she senses in her – tempered, but unfailing. Fernanda wants to know if Kojo can help her find Kudielela.

He explains that he can take the information back to the organisations that help track down missing family members. He writes down a few more details, and then says a sincere '*Obrigado*', thanking them for their time.

Before they go, Kojo gives an encouraging touch to the boy's shoulder, as if to say that he is doing a good job, staying close to his mum.

'You're not the only one looking for somebody,' Kojo says, as Fernanda and the children walk on.

Lena nods. Her stomach twists with shame.

When the family is out of earshot, Kojo speaks harshly. 'You can't just pounce on people like that, Lena. Show some respect, for God's sake!'

She feels like she's been slapped.

'What if she got angry at you, at us?' he continues. 'What if she raised a complaint about CWA? We would not be able to continue to work without acceptance from the people. You don't think, do you?'

Heat rises to her face; she feels she deserves the scorn. But anger and resentment linger as well. Why did he have to say that she's a stranger? Why is she always the one on the outside?

She mumbles her apology, can't explain her conflicting impulses.

They are interrupted by an old man bent over a walking stick coming straight for them. It's not Lena he wants; it's Kojo, where the authority lies.

The man stands shorter than Lena, and she can see rings

73

embedded in his scalp, amongst fuzzy grey hair. His skin hangs off the frail skeleton in a way that makes all the angles harsh and painful to the eye; his collarbone, his elbows, thigh bones all seem too fragile to go on much longer.

The man introduces himself as Okea, a Soba leader. In stumbling Portuguese, he demands to speak to the authorities of the camp. Kojo tries to explain that his team are engineers, not police, but Okea won't be put off. Without pausing for acknowledgement, he stammers on to say that his people will not be forced to march again. The government wants him to move his group to Luremo Sul, but he won't go. It is occupied by UNITA, he says, and the government just want the civilians as human shields. Everyone knows UNITA are holding Luremo as a cover for the diamond mines, he insists. A group of women, children and broken-down old men aren't going to change that.

'I won't lead my people that way,' Okea says. 'We are not going into the mouth of the lion, not for anyone.'

Kojo stands, arms folded, leaning in and concentrating his gaze wholly on Okea's face. The stance shows stability, respect and intense listening. When Kojo asks what he can do to help, Okea is clear: de-mining would get rid of the closest threat, allow the group to settle in and plant before the rainy season.

This is what DJ faced every day, Lena realises. Stories of executions, kidnapping, rape and forced marches. How did she bear it?

She looks at the sun preparing to set. Then her eyes come back to the lines of the water piping leading to the taps, moving gracefully around obstacles. By being useful, that's how.

Kojo says he will take the report to the authorities, and do what he can. He speaks carefully, not making any false promises.

She feels ashamed about how she acted before, wonders how she can change his mind about her.

In the car on the way home, Kojo sits in front and can see her reflection in the mirror. She writes numbers with a chewed pen on the film canisters. She flips through a small notebook, adding details.

He observes her, like watching a bird who might startle. He doesn't like conflict in the team, but he had to speak up. It was an important point about acceptance and treating people with respect. But he doesn't hold onto anger long. Now it has been said the words are out there and he can let it go.

It's interesting, how she was with the camera. She would flit this way and that, as if the creativity made her a bit wild. And she wasn't interested in convention. Out of the corner of his eye, he had seen her on her knees, cheek in the dust, taking photos to include the dramatic sky. Other times her lens was coming over a speaker's shoulder, maybe to see what they were seeing. Towards the end of the day he had let her range a bit further, stepping back to frame the wider scenes from her perspective.

But he can't let her go too far. One step wrong and there could be a landmine. She is his responsibility now.

'Just one thing,' Lena says, out of the blue. 'What about what that FCO guy was talking about? The rumours about nurses poisoning people. Did that come up at all?'

He is taken aback. 'Today? Why do you ask?'

'Is there any truth in it?'

'Of course not.'

'I mean, in people believing it… would it make them afraid?'

'Sometimes rumours do whip people up into a very real fear

that can have an effect on our work. If people thought that our nurses were up to anything sinister...'

'They would stay away,' Jeanette says, her eyes closed. 'I wouldn't have any patients.'

'Would they get angry? Demand an explanation?'

'I don't think so... that's not the Angolan way, usually.'

'Wouldn't they want to know the truth?'

'Sometimes the truth doesn't matter too much, out here,' Jeanette says.

The road is straight and stretches out ahead in long hills. He can tell Lena is tired but still framing the landscape in different ways, holding up her hands as if they were the camera's viewfinder. But eventually it seems as if she is satisfied, and she drops her arms into her lap.

He exhales and wants to stop thinking, worrying and planning. But his mind comes back to what Okea said about Luremo Sul. Maria and DJ ran a clinic there a couple of weeks before the accident. Those two, if they saw something, if something was threatening, why didn't they come to him first? They knew, Maria must have known, that he would have done anything to protect her. Thinking about her is painful. He thought he was long over it, but perhaps that's not the full truth.

There are not many cars, no more checkpoints. Nothing unusual on the road. However, he knows he can never fully relax his state of alertness. Only when he is asleep can he allow that. Even then, you never know.

Fifteen

The noise of the air conditioner shuddering on can't compete with the roar of the generator outside the small building serving as the police station. The air in the waiting room feels stale, cold and stuck. Lena would have much preferred a fan.

Kojo points out the MPLA flag with its red stripe over black, the central yellow star. Below the flag is a framed and faded poster of President dos Santos, staring out with a severe look.

'There's one thing I haven't had the chance to tell you,' Kojo says in a quiet voice. 'We're not really broadcasting that DJ is missing. We wanted to give some time after the accident before everybody started with their questions.'

She doesn't understand, is about to ask why, but the door of the supervisor's office swings open.

'Kojo, my man, no one told me you were waiting!' A man with a gold toothed-smile and a cane holds the door.

'Lena, meet Carlos Macedo, head of the police in Malanje and the surrounding provinces,' Kojo says as they move towards the doorway.

'The pleasure is all mine,' Carlos says, shaking her hand then putting an arm around Kojo. 'Come in, my friend, come in.'

They walk in and the light of the room is the grey-green of

the old fluorescent lighting. It instantly produces a feeling of a closed-off space, lacking all fresh air.

Carlos holds out a silver cigarette holder. 'Kojo, I know you don't have a single vice. Unless something's changed?' Kojo smiles and shakes his head. '*Senhora*, how about you?'

'No thanks.' The smell of cigarette smoke saturates everything: the walls, the fabric on the seats, this man's skin. She is amazed that he needs to light a new one.

Carlos settles into a big boss's chair with a loud squeak of a spring, elbows angled to stabilise himself at the centre of a large desk. She studies his face, and tries to identify what is making her nervous.

With his smooth light-brown skin, high eyebrows and clipped goatee, he is handsome, she assesses. Or was handsome once.

'I'm always happy to have a visit from Kojo,' Carlos says. 'He knows, if it's in my power, I would do anything for this man.'

Kojo murmurs something, too soft for her to hear.

'So what brings you to my humble office?' Carlos asks.

'Lena arrived a couple of days ago in Malanje,' Kojo starts.

'Welcome to Malanje,' Carlos interrupts. 'It's a hell-hole but there are some quality people, I have to say.'

'She's DJ's sister. You remember DJ, the water engineer?' Kojo says.

Carlos rubs his chin for a moment. 'Tall, dark. Living with the nurse from Luremo?'

'Yes, that's the one. The best there is, our DJ. We were wondering how your work has been proceeding looking into the explosion that killed Maria.'

'Such a tragedy,' Carlos says.

'We were there the day before yesterday,' Kojo continues. 'The police tape is still up.'

'You were there? You need to be careful, my friend. You never know what lies beneath the ashes.'

'For Lena's sake.' Kojo looks sideways at her. 'Could you tell us where you are in the investigation?'

'You want to know about the investigation? Well, I have to tell you, it will take some time. But from what we know at this point it seems to be that all signs point to something like a gas leak. Maybe a faulty line into the kitchen. Perhaps someone tinkered with it, siphoning off some for their own use, left it damaged.'

She knows she doesn't understand the context, but it just seems too simple that way. 'Would anyone have held a grudge against them?' she asks. 'For any reason?'

'What do you mean?' Carlos looks surprised.

'It happens, doesn't it?'

'Not very often here. In this place, it feels like a village you know. Everyone knows each other very well. Everyone loved Maria. They wouldn't have wanted her to come to harm.'

'What about this poisoning rumour – would people think nurses were doing harm? Maybe a revenge thing?'

'What? That's preposterous. If you had known Maria you wouldn't dream of saying that.'

'What about DJ? Does everyone love her too?'

Carlos looks quizzically at Kojo, and pauses before he speaks. 'Well, as an outsider, you know –' he grinds his cigarette into the ashtray on his desk – 'some people never really warm to strangers, no matter how long they have been here. Not me, of course. Some small-minded people may have their reservations. But that doesn't turn them into murderers.'

She watches him. His movements are orchestrated to an unusual rhythm as if compensating for something.

'On the night of the explosion,' Carlos says, 'my men came to the accident as fast as we could. But it was clear that the

79

damage was already done. People in the village lined up in a chain to pass buckets of water forward to put out the flames. But it was very slow, as we couldn't go off the paths, with the risk of mines.

'It was too late to save her. That was clear. But people still made an effort for her, for her memory. Not to have everything be lost in the flames.

'One of my men, early on, saw a man running from the area. Everyone else was running towards the house, seeing what they could do to help. But this man was running away. And my men heard a motorcycle start up and move off quickly. Later we realised he had stolen one of our bikes. We haven't had a moment to try to track down the vehicle, with everything else we have to cover.' He waved a hand vaguely over untidy piles of paper on his desk.

'Did you get a description of the man?' she asks.

'No, it was quite a chaotic night.'

'Which way would he have been heading?' She looks to Kojo.

Kojo shrugs. 'This is the first I've heard of a man fleeing the scene.' He turns back to Carlos. 'As I've told you, some of the team members worry that it could have been an attack or a foiled break in, but I can't see it as any more than a tragic accident.'

'And, DJ, she could have also noticed the man fleeing?' she asks.

Looking at Kojo, not Lena, Carlos speaks slowly. 'Yes, it could be possible.'

'Then you have to go after him!' she says, slamming a hand down on the desk's surface. 'He's obviously the prime suspect, isn't he?'

'Hang on, does she know Angola?' Carlos looks sternly at Kojo, as if he has failed to brief his visitor properly. 'Here, you have to be patient. It takes time. If you want to find answers, you may have to wait. Sometimes the answers come to you.'

'And sometimes you have to go looking for them?' she says.

'It depends on how you go about it. The way you act may prevent you from finding what you are looking for.'

She sits back in her chair, humbled. 'Are you looking for this motorcycle man, or do you expect him to come to you?'

'Me? I have an open mind, young lady. I have to, in this job. I also know that sometimes fate acts in a way that we wish wasn't an accident, but it may prove to be just that.'

'And if it wasn't an accident?'

'Then I have to proceed with a good head on my shoulders, you know. People usually make a slip up. Often times a part of them may want to be found. If they do not want to be found, then it is very difficult.' Carlos gets up from his chair. 'I wish I could do more to help you, I really do.'

Kojo moves to open the door. 'Thank you for your time, Carlos. Please radio us if there is any news. About any of it. We really appreciate it.'

'Of course my friend. You have my word.'

Friend. Does that word do justice to what they have been through? Kojo moves out of the office as he has many times before after a meeting. But each time he leaves the place he feels a jolt. Like an electric shock, stinging him and bringing him back to that moment two years ago.

There was that emergency SOS call for any medical first responder, saying that the head of police had been in an accident. No time to transmit any more information.

CWA's car was available and Jeanette jumped to the call. Sebastião drove and Kojo came too, in case there were multiple casualties.

What they had found wasn't a surprise. Landmine incidents were so common that they should have been used to them, but somehow when it was someone they knew, it made it physically painful to approach the scene. It could have been us, could have been our car, he thought. There but for the grace of God go I.

What was unusual was that the MPLA anti-landmine protection undercarriage had failed so spectacularly. They bet their lives on that protection, and yet this one had shattered in the face of what seemed to be a normal landmine. Had it been tampered with?

Someone had pulled Carlos out of the burnt chassis, which still smoked not far from where he lay on the road. He was screaming, twisting in pain and reaching for his leg. From where they were, it looked like a burnt log, splintered and cut short. A crowd of villagers circled around but held themselves at a distance.

'Hang on in there, Carlos!' Jeanette shouted as she jumped out of the car before Sebastião brought it to a complete stop. She pushed through the line of onlookers and ran to him. She had her medic bag across her chest and open to find the IVs even before she had reached him. She sank to her knees on the tarmac next to him. 'Hold on there, darlin'. You'll be all right, we'll make it all right.'

There were no other victims. Why no driver? A man in his position would always have a driver. Very odd.

Kojo stood close to Jeanette and waited for instructions. He was the team leader, but in this kind of situation her medical knowledge put her entirely in charge. She was moving faster than he had ever seen her. Her hands stopped only momentarily to take his pulse from the wrist, then kept moving.

Carlos was moaning and had his eyes closed. But when she

ripped back his trousers to see the exposed bones and shreds of skin, he opened up his eyes and mouth, sat up and let out a scream for mercy.

'Hold him,' she ordered Kojo. He obeyed by crouching down behind him, propping the man up. It was an awkward pose and there must have been a better way to do it, but he couldn't figure where to best put himself as Carlos thrashed and shook.

Jeanette rolled back the sleeve and gave Carlos an injection that calmed him. She inserted the IV next, holding it in place while using her teeth to cut the surgical tape. 'He still has the knee, that's lucky.' She worked quickly to keep the wound moist and clean enough to be transported to hospital. 'Much better than it could have been.'

Carlos sank back, giving his weight to Kojo.

Lucky he still has the knee. The words have stayed with Kojo and come back to him when he thinks of what to be grateful for in this God forsaken place.

That kind of experience changes you. When you hold a man's back against your chest, your arms wrapped around him to keep him stable, and you feel his howl go down to a whimper. You feel his heart beating so fast, trying to pump blood up from a leg that's no longer there. You feel the adrenaline shooting through his body as the flight-or-flight instinct short-circuits. He is terrified that he might never go anywhere again but heaven or hell, and you are holding him in your arms like a wounded brother.

That changes you, and changes him. Something between you is exchanged without your consent. And both of you will always be marked by that.

Sixteen

The women who open the door recognise you. They wear white habits that frame their faces like perfect cathedral windows. They look down and don't meet your eyes as they allow you in.

They know. You know they know. It's in the shape of their mouths, although nothing is mentioned. That's what drew you here. The assumption of silence. No one will make you talk.

You look a mess. Haven't changed clothes since the accident. A day's motorcycle ride hasn't blown anything clear. You smell of sweat, smoke and blood.

They give you a room. Just a small room for one. Clean sheets. Simple clothes to wear. You appreciate the soft old cotton trousers and shirt.

You take a sponge bath in a dark cubicle. Holes carved in the shape of a crucifix let in the late-afternoon sunlight. The water is cold, and the soap stings your cuts, but you scrub harder. You want some physical sensation as an excuse for the pain you feel inside. Tears run down your face as you crouch down in a squat, raking your naked back roughly on the concrete wall. Words are impossible now, but groans and sobs escape you and echo away.

Seventeen

'What was DJ like as a child?' Kojo asks at dinner.

'Oh, she was always in motion,' Lena says. 'Couldn't keep still to save her life. The only thing that gave her some kind of focus was her judo class. Mum signed her up from the age of eleven or so. DJ was brilliant at it.'

She pauses to see if anyone wants her to stop, but no one seems to.

'I'm eight years younger. I watched her judo competitions with awe, but they weren't for me. We were close, you wouldn't expect it with the age difference, but it's true. She always had a way of looking after me without making me feel like I was a burden.

'But DJ had a lot of anger when she was young. Had a temper that could fly off in any direction. At our mum, a lot. At the church. Righteous anger, you know. She channelled it, I guess.'

She stops. She doesn't want to tell them how that temper used to take away all the air in the room. Forced you to turn around and pay attention only to what DJ wanted. Everyone had to stop everything they were doing to deal with whatever it was that set her off.

'It's just her and me as family since Mum died, and Dad eighteen months before her,' she continues. 'It seems as if she really polished up, turning into a team leader here, organising all the engineers. It's so impressive what you do.'

She is ashamed to feel that she might cry, but doesn't know why.

She looks away from them and instead focuses on some of the personal details around the place. She sees a plaque made of plant cloth expressing thanks to CWA for a project. Crockery of different shapes and patterns lies haphazardly in the drying tray near the sink. Photos of the team are tacked to the walls.

She stands up to get closer to a group picture.

'Is that DJ?' she asks.

In the photo DJ looks different. Her hair is shaved close at the sides and longer at the top, coming down over one eye. She is laughing, with one arm dangling casually over a woman's shoulder. The way she holds herself, with shoulders rounded forward, seems both humble and quietly confident. DJ is next to a woman who looks not at the camera but sideways. The camera catches her mouth open with laughter. The woman is beautiful, with smooth coffee-coloured skin and black curly hair flowing long. DJ looks sturdy and taut, handsome like a man.

That night, Kojo hears a scream coming from the front room. Jumping up, he is out of bed and at her door.

'Lena, are you all right?'

His knocks push the door open.

She is not awake. He catches her in the middle of a restless dream, something that can't be resolved. Her legs are moving quickly as if she is trying to run. Her breathing is fast and her arms are fidgeting. She twists her head from side to side as if to avoid something. Her mouth is open and trying to speak. Strands of hair are caught in the corners and can't break free.

Her face looks beautiful to him, even in distress. He smells her scent of sleep and it jars him. It is too intimate.

But she needs help. Would it be better to interrupt the dream or let it run its course?

He puts out a hand to her arm to try to urge her awake. As he makes contact with the skin he feels her heat and the stickiness of sweat.

She throws off his touch and remains in her nightmare. She is constant movement, twisting and trembling.

Suddenly, she screams again so loudly that she snaps awake. Legs drop. All the frenetic motion stops as the scream echoes around the walls of the bare room.

He is so close that it hurts his ears, and he has to move back.

She sits up and turns on the light. She puts her hands to her mouth, blinking with the light and surprise. The strands of hair are still there, moist with saliva. Her t-shirt is thin, showing the angles of her shoulders and the shape of her breasts.

She sees him. 'What happened?' she asks, with a childlike acceptance of the merging of dreams and reality.

'I think it might have been a Larium dream,' he says. 'Is this the day you take your malaria medicine? Vivid dreams can be a side effect. Are you all right?'

She nods slowly. Then she rubs her face with both hands over her eyes in a circular motion, moving down over her cheekbones to her jaw and her neck, with a big exhale. 'Was that my scream?'

'Yes, but don't worry about it. It happens sometimes.'

'Sorry to wake you.'

'No,' he lies. 'I was just in the kitchen and knocked on your door.' He tries to come up with something else to say. Something to comfort her, or to ease her back to sleep, but he can't think of anything that feels right. He has a terrible urge to kiss her, but he barely knows the woman and who knows where that would lead to.

The room feels small, too close.

'Well, good night,' Kojo says as he leaves the room, and pulls the door closed behind him.

Part II

Eighteen

Car headlights turn outside the villa, shining a curve across the dining table.

'*Senhor Kojo!*' It's Angelo, the night watchman. '*Táxi não marcado!*'

'Expecting anyone?' Kojo looks around. The others shake their heads.

The car doesn't cut the engine. It reverses soon after the passenger disembarks and the lights swing away again.

'*É ok, Angelo,*' Kojo says quietly as he opens the screen door.

In walks the FCO man from the Greek place a couple of nights before. He is still wearing the expensive suit, rumpled from the heat. He holds himself tall with that public–schoolboy confidence that you can see from miles away.

The blond hair and ginger eyebrows are pleasant enough, but she knows his type, him and boys like him. They come from places like Hampstead, Chelsea, even from Stockwell, but not her corner of Stockwell. Not her concrete three-layer estate with the dripping rain, the rubbish and the packs of kids scrabbling to work out who comes out on top. No, he isn't her kind at all. Her shoulders and whole body retreat away from him.

'Everyone, this is Jake Lansdowne,' says Kojo. He turns back to the visitor. 'What's going on?'

'You know about the WFP flight? Shot at, nearly shot down?' Jake says. They shake their heads. 'Somehow UNITA have picked up a surface-to-air weapon big enough to make the last WFP pilot turn back. They've called off all landings at Malanje until further notice. So I need a place to sleep for a night or two, if that's all right with you. Kojo, my good man, you had mentioned that you have a spare room…?'

'Nope, sorry lad,' Jeanette says. 'Lena's in it.'

'We have a sofa, however,' Kojo says. 'If that is acceptable to you?'

'If there are no flights,' Jake says, 'what choice do I have? A sofa would be delightful. Thank you so much.'

The news hits her. No more flights. Cut off from Luanda. Lifeline out of here, back to normal life, London, gone.

'How long do they stop the flights?' she asks, looking to Kojo.

'They do this sometimes,' he says slowly. 'Usually they lift the flight ban after forty-eight hours or so.'

'Not sure about that this time, mate,' says Jake. 'I've been studying UNITA for a long time and they've never pulled out hardware like this. They would've kept it hidden for a rainy day or something special, like the president's private jet.'

'But no movements until the flights get going again,' Jeanette says quietly.

'No ex-pat movements, that's for sure,' Jake says.

'Even medical?' Lena asks.

'Even everything, sweetheart,' Jake says. She makes a face and looks away. She wishes she knew more about the situation than this guy.

'Our supplies are fine for about two weeks,' calculates Kojo, looking at the ceiling to concentrate. 'But if an emergency comes up we will have to radio SOS for a helicopter, I suppose. UNITA have never shot down a medical helicopter before.'

'There's always a first time,' Jake says.

Brad is drawn into the conversation and invites Jake to relax with a beer. Jake offers strong opinions on the state of the conflict, and the recent political changes. He seems to be a self-appointed expert on rebel movements and diamonds smuggled from the conflict zones. He calls them blood diamonds, as if he is a journalist doing an exposé, and talks as if *The Times* has already granted him a front-page story.

'Have you seen anything unusual?' Jake asks. 'Profiteering? More than the usual, I hasten to add.'

'Some people are making a shit-load of money off this war,' Brad says. 'Always have been. They recruit kids and villagers to do their dirty work. They don't give a rat's ass about how many thousands have malaria or typhoid from the water or whatever.'

'But we care,' Lena says.

'Of course we do. You do, and you just got here.'

'Brad,' Jeanette says. 'Don't be a prat.'

'Okay, okay. But it's true. I work my ass off here seven days a week, setting up water tanks and moving supplies, and why do I do it? Because I care about keeping people alive. But if the leaders don't give a shit, who am I? A fool.'

'But,' says Jake, 'if you could find out where the diamonds were going, wouldn't that change things?' He puts his beer down on the floor, weaves his hands together to make a loud crack down the line of knuckles. 'My sources say there has been a lot more of a rush lately to cash in while they can.' He looks around. 'Have you noticed anything? Anyone especially jumpy or in more of a hurry than usual?'

She thinks back to the government troops manning the roadblock. They didn't seem to be in a hurry. As if time for them had stopped meaning anything. Maybe Jake doesn't know everything, not quite.

'And then these rumours I was picking up.' Jake gestures to Kojo. 'About the villagers being afraid that nurses are poisoning people. Don't you see, that just drives them away from the establishment, and towards the rebels?'

'It's a bit arrogant,' Jeanette says, 'to assume that people could be easily tricked into refusing medical treatment from someone they trust.'

'You know this place, rumours spread faster than influenza!' For some reason Jake finds this funny and chortles. 'Possibly the rebels are running out of time,' he continues. 'That would lead to lots of uncoordinated movements, some counterintuitive or counterproductive. But overall this stirring up of the hive, and all this activity of people trying to control the movements of more and more people and diamonds before—'

'Before...?' Kojo asks.

'Who knows? Angola can always surprise us, no?' He slaps both hands on his knees and laughs again, sounding forced. 'Anyone have a fag?'

'I've got cigarettes, if that's what you mean,' Brad says. 'We'll go outside, so not to disturb y'all.' The two men continue their conversation in murmurs out of earshot, on the veranda.

'Seen him before,' Jeanette says to no one in particular. She takes the dinner dishes to the sink and looks blankly out of the window into the black outside. 'Before Maria died. Something about him...'

'I think he's all right,' Kojo says. 'It might be good for us to help an FCO contact.' He pauses and then adds, 'I'm going to check in with security and hear more about the situation with WFP.' He takes the broken stairs two at a time to reach the radio communications room.

*

'And where are you from?' asks Jake when he comes back inside. It is the first time he's acknowledged Lena.

'South London. Stockwell. You?'

He holds his hands up, palms showing. 'Not a Londoner, I'm afraid. From Devon originally. I like London though. Was in Pimlico before this posting.' He studies her face, narrowing his eyes. 'But where are you from, originally?'

She hesitates, thinking back to Lucien and the others growing up on the estate. 'My parents are Portuguese, if that's what you mean,' she says. 'But I was born in King's College Hospital, where my mum worked until the day she died.'

'My cousin married a Portuguese girl,' he says. 'Lovely woman. Holiday romance. Together they've opened a ring of villas off the coast in Madeira. Get back there much?' he asks.

'Not in years,' she says, slipping out of the room as soon as she possibly can.

Kojo watches her leave. He senses her unease about Jake, doesn't know the roots of it. He coolly reserves judgement. After years in this business he has spent time with many characters of varying shades of shiftiness. Each with their own agenda, convinced it is hidden. Thinking their lies won't catch up with them.

Jake could be useful to them, Kojo feels. But that doesn't mean he likes the man. He has got to where he is by being respectful, but closed on any real level to these strangers with their unspoken expectations and demands. Ex-pats out for a short time. Strangers here with no depth, slippery and not worth the trust.

It's different for an African living outside of his home

country. He is Ghanaian first and finally. He can blend in with the national staff, but has the observations of an outsider. The acceptance of a local but the privileges of a diplomat. It is as if he speaks all their languages at the same time, and can hear what's underneath the cacophony.

And he doesn't like how Jake was relating to the team, and to Lena. As if he already knows her. As if she might owe him something.

He remembers now that there was something before with Jake and DJ. In a previous visit to Malanje, they seemed like they were going to meet up, but then it was disrupted. He never heard the full story. DJ was too angry about it – some insult or another – for him to get to the bottom of what happened.

Sooner rather than later he would like to see Jake out of the villa. This is his team, his family to all intents and purposes. He needs to protect that.

But for now, he mixes in with the people he leads. The two white men down a few beers each and their volume increases as the evening progresses. They do not notice how they dominate the atmosphere with their wide gestures and honking laughs. They continue to talk loudly, long after the women have gone to bed.

Kojo observes. He gleans from the newcomer that he was up north in Luremo recently. Although Jake avoids saying it directly, it seems as if he's had a few trips to the provinces on the border in quick succession, as if he feels he is on the verge of a breakthrough.

Nineteen

Lena jumps out of her sleep at the roar of the engines approaching – cars, how many? What's going on? Where's Angelo? Isn't anyone on night watch?

Car doors slam, engines still running. Heavy boots moving fast. She doesn't know whether to come out of her room or to hide within. She hears the swishes of soft tread moving inside the villa. Someone jumps down the staircase taking many steps at a time.

A huge male voice pounds through the front door. '*Senhor* Lansdowne, we know you are in there!' She feels the sun-warped wood could split away.

Kojo's voice holds a forced calm. '*Quem está lá fora?*'

The voice outside hammers back, '*Este é o MPLA. Queremos interrogar o* Lansdowne.'

She opens her bedroom door to see Kojo, Brad and Jeanette huddled together near the front door. They are in their sleepwear: Brad in boxers, Jeanette in a long t-shirt. Kojo has an African printed wrap around his waist, chest bare. Jake is standing slim and tall against the door frame to the living room. She can't see his face, just a silhouette. The headlights outside shine through the front windows despite the curtains, making eerie squares of shadow and light.

'They want you for questioning,' Kojo says to Jake. 'It's MPLA, regional officers. Are you in trouble?'

'There must be some mistake,' Jake says in an urgent whisper, not moving.

'A mistake that's called out three armoured vehicles?'

Jake lifts his hands up like an innocent man. 'Well… I may have asked too many questions.'

'Questions?'

'The blood diamonds file. And, you know… the MPLA interests.'

'Go on…'

'As we said –' Jake's face darts around, looking for support from Brad – 'there are profits in this war, some people get hacked off if those are threatened.'

'They wouldn't storm a CWA house,' Kojo says, 'but they seem really angry.'

'Can't you do something? You know Carlos, can't you get them to back off?'

Kojo looks at Jake like a child needing reprimand. 'I can't do that, Jake. We don't do stand-offs.'

Jake says nothing, frozen in his stance.

'We must keep good relationships with the authorities.' Kojo takes a deep breath and turns towards the door.

Lena wishes, for his sake, that he had his professional clothes on, but there's no time. At least the men will see he is unarmed.

He opens the front door. The man who had pounded before has gone back to one of the cars. The beams from the headlights shine a direct glare that traces Kojo's head, chest and hips. In a slow smooth gesture he holds both hands up. To Lena, he seems in that one movement to be both heroic and totally vulnerable.

As the men see the colour of his skin and who he is, they will know they do not have the man they want. Kojo walks with steady deliberate steps towards the cars.

Several minutes pass. Nothing can be heard over the engines rattling.

Jeanette hisses, 'If anything happens to Kojo...'

Brad says, 'Nothing's going to happen to Kojo. He can handle it.'

Jake says nothing.

Lena walks quietly towards the others who are still huddled by the front door.

Jeanette reaches and puts her arm around Lena. She is soft and plump, smelling of mosquito repellent. 'It'll be all right,' she says.

A few minutes later, Kojo comes back inside. 'They want to take you in,' he says. Jake doesn't move from the shadows, as if he wants to blend in with the wood.

'They say you have problems with your visa,' Kojo continues. 'This must be big. Carlos is leading it personally, as head of the MPLA police in all the northern provinces.'

'Carlos Macedo,' Jeanette says under her breath. 'That's a man I haven't seen in a long time.'

'I don't have to go with them, do I?' Jake says. 'Can't I, can't we work something out?'

'Does the FCO know you are here?' Kojo asks, pulling Jake by the elbow into the dimly lit hallway. 'If so, then you can radio the embassy straight away and set this right.'

Jake's face crumples. 'Not exactly. It's for a story. For *The Sunday Times,* you see. They're interested in the diamonds, and how they fuel the war. When this goes to print it's really going to make my name. So I sort of had to pursue it...'

'...On your own,' Kojo says. He studies the man's face for a moment. 'This visit is off the record, is it?'

Jake twitches his chin to agree.

'But you are a British citizen? Is that bit true?'

This time he nods vigorously, as if he senses his Britishness will save him nevertheless.

'Then the British Embassy has to look after you. They won't let the MPLA disappear you.'

Jake sets his shoulders square, as if he wants to hide that his worst fears have been voiced.

The noise outside grows as they rev the engines.

'I think I've done all I can. I've got guarantees for your safe passage, if you go now. Anyone British can press your case with the embassy. All international political prisoners have certain rights.'

Kojo seems to see Lena for the first time in the half-light, his expression troubled. 'You have a British passport, right?'

Everyone looks at her.

'I hate to do this to you, but how would you feel about going with him?'

She pulls back from the question. Jeanette's arm around her squeezes tighter.

'Kojo, she's just a child!' Jeanette says.

'I'm not,' Lena says, not sure of what she is being asked to do. 'But I don't know him, or his situation.'

'You're a citizen. You have access to the British Embassy and they have to listen to you.'

'But, I want to be here, with the team,' she says. 'I need to find DJ! And… who is he? He's this arrogant guy, walking in here, assuming that we'll bail him out.'

'If you don't want to go,' Jake says, 'we can't make you.'

Kojo's eyes hold hers for a moment. 'No, we can't make you,' he says slowly. 'But sometimes we have the chance to help people, help one person. Even if it is someone who we may not like very much.'

She looks from Kojo to Brad to Jeanette to Jake. Is Kojo telling her the whole story? Or has something been agreed in the back of those cars or restaurants between the whispers of men?

'And anyway, I can't spare a member of the team,' Kojo continues. 'With Maria gone and the situation with DJ... we do not have any extra capacity, I'm afraid.'

'I see,' she says. 'All right Jake, I'll go with you to Luanda and make sure the British know where you are. But then, as soon as the flights start up again, I'd like to come right back. Is that okay, Kojo?'

He exhales. 'Yes, you have my word.'

'And you have guarantees we'll be safe?'

'Nothing will bother you, not in those vehicles. And Carlos is a good man, you met him yourself. He owes CWA – we saved his life in a landmine accident once.'

'We're driving to Luanda?'

'It will be long,' Kojo says. 'Collect your things. I'll go and tell the drivers.'

'I'll rustle up some food and water bottles,' Jeanette says, scurrying to the kitchen.

Jake stays still a moment longer. His mouth is drawn tight and small.

Lena looks at him. 'Well?' she says, hands on her hips.

'Thank you,' he says quietly.

The three cars are in a line, driving down the middle of the dirt road. No one seems to be coming from the other direction, so they barrel forward unimpeded.

Jake and Lena are in the middle vehicle. Their view is restricted by lots of metal over the windows and windscreen, probably for protection against landmines. The lead vehicle ahead rides higher than the others, with even more undercarriage protection.

The driver says nothing. He wears a government uniform of dark green, some patches indicating honours earned. The radio plays West African music and Portuguese love songs, broken only by hourly news spurts, with repeated statements about President dos Santos and the MPLA winning against the rebels. Carlos wears the government uniform and sits in the passenger seat. He has said nothing since they climbed in.

Hours pass. She leans her head against the window and watches a dry red landscape move past. She is going in the exact opposite direction to the one she should be.

What would DJ do in this situation? Would she help someone just because it seemed like she could? What would Mum do? That's obvious. She helped anybody. Didn't need a reason.

She looks over to see Jake sleeping, head back, mouth slightly ajar. She wishes she liked him more, but something in her cannot.

He wakes with a snort and shakes his head to open his eyes. He catches her looking at him and cocks a smile. Opening a water bottle, he says, 'Here's looking at you, kid.'

'I'm sorry about what I said before,' she says.

'It's okay. Sometimes people feel that way about me.'

She doesn't say it is untrue. 'It wasn't kind though. Sorry.'

'Maybe this little jaunt will change your mind.' He smiles. His confidence is back, with the sunlight and the moving car.

'If you have a plan,' she whispers to him, 'you might want to let me know what it is.'

He puts his fingers to his lips and gestures to the officers' backs. He slips a notebook and pen out of his bag and writes, then hands the pad to her.

No plan. He grins and raises his eyebrows, and starts whistling a tune that no one could possibly like.

The cars pull into Luanda. It's near sunset; they've been driving all night and most of the day. Only took two breaks, when they refilled the petrol with containers from the boot. Lena was told to relieve herself behind the wheels of the last car. The men turned their backs to look away. No peeing off route, she knows. Mines potentially present, everywhere.

A battered sign announces *Hotel Luz do Sol.* The fluorescent sign flickers, unsteady. The short hotel is pinched between two tall ones that could have been built in competition. They are all in the shadow of several silver skyscrapers, some half-finished, boasting and flashy.

'Your hotel,' Carlos announces, gesturing to her to get out of the car. The engine keeps running.

'What happens to him?' she asks.

'We'll take care of him,' Carlos says quietly, not removing his broad dark glasses.

'But you promised,' Jake says, panic in his voice. 'Kojo said…'

'You won't be harmed,' Carlos's voice rumbles, as if that isn't his wish. 'The British Mission will be expecting her in the morning.'

She searches Jake's face, telling him with a shake of her head that they don't have a choice. But she tries to instil in him some confidence, that she'll be there. She gathers her overnight bag and gets out of the car.

It moves off before her door is fully shut. The last thing she sees is Carlos reaching diagonally back to pull it closed from the inside.

Twenty

The British Embassy operates out of the top floors of a dilapidated block of flats in Luanda's city centre. It is marked by a paper Union Jack held to the inside of the window with peeling Sellotape.

Two fans oscillate around the waiting room, where the walls seem to sag with the penetrating heat. Posters for oil companies brighten up the walls with their lime green and sunshine orange. There is another *No Cameras* sign, and a framed picture of the Queen. A strongly worded announcement gives notice about the yellow fever vaccine requirement. Another poster has a photo of a woman with her face hidden, asking *How much can YOU trust your sexual partner?* A bowl of free condoms sits on a table below, their silver- and gold-coloured wrappers dulled by the fluorescent lights. Nobody takes one.

Lena doesn't have much hope after more than an hour and a half in the waiting room. In the form enquiring about Jake, she had to leave most of the details blank.

Her name is called, and she is ushered behind the thickened glass into a corridor closed off from all windows. She walks behind an Angolan member of staff with elaborate plaits whirling up to a large bun fixed to the top of her head. She is dressed in fine African cloth and moves with a grace that says that she, and only she, will decide where they shall stop.

Many doors come off to the left and the right. Slits of the Angolan noon-bright sun slip under each threshold. Towards the end of the corridor the woman slows and reaches for a door handle. 'You will wait in here.'

Lena has to blink and squint. Floor-to-ceiling glass makes up one wall, the others are paper-white and look about as flimsy. The room is small with a round table and chairs with peeling coverings. As her eyes adjust she sees that from the sixth floor there is a wide panoramic view of the city. There are thousands upon thousands of blocks of flats. Some are finished and populated, satellite dishes crowding the flat roofs. Others are only half constructed, with iron poles sticking out in different directions and hollow concrete rooms atop the bottom layers. All are occupied at street level with shops or businesses, and you can sense that families or groups are living above, despite the fact that the buildings are unfinished: lines of laundry flicker with clothing in different sizes, cooking pots tipped upside down in the sun to air-dry.

The sunlight is flat and harsh, and there are few shadows to hide behind. The colours are bleached versions of themselves. Beyond the flats rise up slums, with their own broken geometry of cardboard boxes, muted colours and improvised roofs. As she leans closer to try to see details, the door opens.

A white woman wearing a rumpled suit jacket and pencil skirt comes into the room. Her hair is falling out of her ponytail. Her face looks red and uncomfortable. The papers in her hand are askew and threatening to tumble onto the floor. She doesn't look much older than Lena, but tasked with heavier responsibilities. She introduces herself as Miss Cartwright, and takes a drink from a water bottle before pressing the papers into some kind of order on the table.

As the woman silently skims the papers, Lena wonders what she is supposed to do. She tries to look for new information, reading upside down, but they are just the forms she herself submitted.

'And what is your relation to Mr Lansdowne?' Miss Cartwright looks up at her with purple bags under her eyes. Lena wonders if she was trained not to believe people on first contact.

'No relation. An acquaintance, really. We met in Malanje.'

She flips through the papers. 'You've known him for…'

'About thirty-six hours.'

'And you're willing to vouch for him?'

Lena nods, not fully convinced herself.

'Why? What is he to you?'

'Nothing. I don't know him, not well. But my team leader, Kojo Appiah, the director of CWA, he put his word on it that Jake would not go and be… unaccounted for. So I was volunteered to be here.'

'Well, the Angolans have gone and locked him up. You're not family, so I can't guarantee access. And I have to see with the FCO if they recognise his profile.' She quickly skims the pages at the bottom of her pile. 'But I think I can press the authorities for Jake to have a visitor, to make sure nothing bad has happened. The best scenario would be that he is swiftly deported, you know that, right? The worst scenario…' She trails off and writes some notes in the margins of the last page.

'Come back after two,' she says, brushing back the strands of hair that had escaped from her ponytail. 'I'll see what I can do.'

'Thank you.' Lena catches her eye on leaving, which forces the woman to give her a small smile. It may be the first time she's smiled all day.

Twenty-one

The guard leads Lena down a dark corridor of bare concrete. The daylight through the gate fades quickly as they walk. The way is lit only by sparse bare bulbs that shine with a green and lifeless hue. The place reeks of sewage and trapped air. Her breath is uneven as she tries not to inhale too deeply.

She has to half-run to keep up with the guard. She is on the edge of a world she has no desire to enter. Never has been close. Lucien told her what it was like in Brixton prison when he was held there, for the third time caught spraying his tag on the estate. Wasn't too long, lucky they judged him in the end as a minor even though he was almost eighteen. Said he'd never go back there. One of thousands of boys all minimised to a point where you could even forget your reason for living, he'd said. He was changed a bit by that time inside. After that, he was less boastful. More cautious. Still Lucien though. You could depend on that.

This place, what would Lucien think of it? Poor Jake, held for visa irregularities, or so they said. She swallows hard when she thinks about her own forged letter. She tries to erase any trace of guilt from her face. Surely no one is going to look back at that signature on a piece of paper held in London, are they?

107

The prison's sharp geometry repels her, as does the stench. She pulls in her shoulders tight near her neck. She senses the bodies incarcerated in small spaces, powerless against the angles and the concrete. She resents Jake yet again, for getting into this mess and needing her help, making her come into contact with all of this.

She knows she should have sympathy for someone held behind these walls, but this visit feels like punishment for a crime she hasn't committed. The smells transform into a taste at the back of her throat that makes her gag silently. She can't lose pace though, the guard shows no sign of slowing.

Regime de isolamento, the sign announces as they enter a different part of the prison. The guard flips through a rusted ring of keys. There is the sound of water dripping, and occasional groans from different directions. She can't tell which is the original noise and which the echo. Or is it a call and response? The noises retreat, come back, intrude into her mind.

The guard stops in front of a cell no different from the others. There is a wooden flap, above Lena's eye level, which he shifts to see who is inside. He grunts confirmation.

The door groans to the side in a heavy movement. Inside, Jake sits on the edge of a metal bed frame, no mattress. His torso, looking too large for the space, is bent over his knees, head in his hands. His suit jacket is rolled into a wrinkled ball for a pillow. His shirt is streaked with brown sweat stains. Patches of dried blood have clotted in his blond hair near his left temple. Purple blotches mark his face and dark circles ring his eyes. His square jaw is swollen on one side.

She takes a deep breath. She wishes she had her camera with her to document this moment, rather than having to act in it. She's never faced a look like this one before: expectant, hurt, but still determined. She can tell by the way his eyes drift over her that he is not pleased it's only her. He was hoping for someone else. Someone with the authority to overrule the decision to keep him here.

She looks around at the cracked walls, the high barred window peering out to a patch of strangled daylight. There is a cracked pot in the corner swarming with insects. She thinks about diarrhoea and malaria, and the thoughts pull her mouth out of shape before she realises it. She tries to hide her reaction, bury it back down.

'Did you talk to the ambassador?' Jake asks with a sudden jolt of energy.

'I was at the embassy this morning.' She tries to put more enthusiasm into her voice than she feels. 'They've opened up a new file on you. But the fact that the FCO didn't know you were back in the country made it a bit harder.'

'Yah, well… I should've probably told you about my other passport. Swiss, from my mum's side.'

'Why'd you come back, Jake?' she asks. 'If you knew you were pissing people off this badly?'

He looks around at the walls and shakes his head, gesturing as if invisible speakers will pick up their words.

'Do you want me to contact a lawyer or someone?'

He chews the inside of his cheek. 'Not yet,' he says slowly. 'I think the embassy will come round to seeing that I'm not in the wrong here.'

She stands back. He tries to demand a level of respect which he simply hasn't earned. But you don't kick a man when he's down.

Instead, she asks, 'Is there anything you need? Are they giving you food and water? Is it clean?'

He shakes his head in a yes–no kind of way.

'The embassy said I should give you this.' She hands him a water bottle and a vial of iodine tablets for later. 'Don't put too much in, mind, or you could poison yourself.'

He accepts the gifts, but his expression says he was expecting more.

'Do you want me to try to get a doctor in here? Or the Red Cross?'

'Just get me out of here,' he growls, like an animal too big for the cage but tired from the fight.

She takes a taxi back to her hotel before sunset. She feels crumpled. It is exhausting to try to navigate the stiff logic of another country's laws and procedures, translated through Miss Cartwright and the prison officials. She wants to get back to her hotel room, to wash the smell of prison off her. To lie naked and clean on the bed with a fan oscillating. But that's just the body. What to do with all these disturbing images in the mind? Jake being beaten. Okea's people being pushed into a minefield. Fernanda's sister being kidnapped. Maria caught in the explosion.

At the hotel she pays the driver his kwanzas and he speeds off in a whirl of dust.

She looks up to the sky. A large plane is coming into land at Luanda's airport. What will it take to convince a pilot to fly out to Malanje once again?

Twenty-two

Jake lifts his hair at the temple to show a shaved patch with some stitches. 'A doctor visited and fixed me up with some antibiotics and painkillers.' He stands up from the metal bed and gestures for her to take a seat, but she shakes her head.

She tells him how, at the embassy, they have been pressing to reduce the charge to irregular entry into the country. 'The Angolans were much more extreme at first, Jake, carrying on about espionage charges. We've tried to calm everything down. The penalty looks likely to be deportation and the payment of their legal expenses. And you'll have to sign an affidavit stating what your purpose of travel was.'

He raises his eyebrows. 'And if I refuse to sign?'

She sighs. 'Then you're not as clever as I thought.'

He grunts. 'Listen.' He beckons her closer. 'These people,' he whispers, 'they want me rubbed out.'

'You think so? Really? Then why haven't they done it already?'

'Because I have connections, see.' He gestures around as if these people surround him. 'People would notice, and they would talk. It wouldn't look good if a British official was knocked down, would it?'

'British ex-official,' she reminds him.

'British ex-official who is about to break the story!' His head nods vigorously with confidence.

'What story?'

'You know, who is siphoning the diamonds out of Malanje, the person on the inside making it happen.'

'On the inside?'

'You don't think the small local UNITA blokes and sorry conscripts are the whole story, do you? They need a leader, someone driving this thing. And a method of transport,' he says. 'My money's on the local MPLA, maybe working with the pilots.'

'The MPLA? Why would they want to do business with the rebels?'

'I was trying to get someone trusted on the inside to talk to me… But she didn't want to cooperate in the end.' He smirks. 'Her loss.'

'*Acabou o tempo!*' The guard shouts. The door slides open again roughly and he gestures with a nod that she must go.

'Anything else you want me to say to the embassy?'

'Tell them I owe them one,' he says.

'You may owe them more than that,' she says.

'See you tomorrow.'

The third time Lena visits the embassy, Miss Cartwright doesn't keep her waiting. She is wearing the same creased suit and looks as though she may have slept under her desk. Lena resists the urge to reach out and tuck the stray wisps into the ever-present ponytail.

'Jake hasn't done himself any favours, you know,' Miss Cartwright says.

'I don't exactly love him at this moment,' Lena says. 'I need to get back to the highlands and he's keeping me here.'

'The ink hadn't even dried on his dismissal forms from the FCO when he came back here, using the other passport. That's a perfect way to get the Angolans' backs up, acting like you think you're smarter than they are.'

'But in Malanje he was still describing himself as FCO. He has *cojones*, that's for sure.'

That gets a smile from Miss Cartwright. Not a big smile, but a recognisable one. 'Yes, and arrogance. But no one deserves ill-treatment. They should never have touched him in prison. They should have known we would hear about it. It's become a bit of an incident, I'm afraid. The ambassador has made a statement. The Angolans have agreed for him to be released to take the Brussels Airlines Saturday flight in three days' time. But he'll be blacklisted. I don't think he'd be allowed into any West African country now – their border security is all linked, you see.'

'That's really helpful.' Lena leans closer to her. 'He'll get out of here and then neither of us will have to deal with him again. You've been so brilliant, really you have.' She pauses, while she considers whether she should tell her more. 'Can I ask your first name?'

Miss Cartwright stiffens, but then sees no reason to refuse. 'It's Charlotte.'

'How long have you been in Angola, Charlotte?'

'Eighteen months. My fiancé is acting deputy ambassador at the moment. We're hoping for a European posting next, closer to home.'

Lena nods, as if this is an understandable goal to strive for. 'Charlotte, can I ask you something? Have you heard anything about an explosion in Malanje? In January?'

'Why, were British citizens hurt?'

'No, I don't think so. But it's something I heard about when I was there. I was wondering if it was on your radar.'

'I don't cover the north. My portfolio is citizen's affairs.' Charlotte shrugs. 'If it's a local thing, then we rely on the government or the aid agencies to report it to us. We get things second- or third-hand. Was it something significant?' Her face is animated for the first time.

'I don't know yet,' Lena says. 'It set off a cascade of events I'm trying to unravel.' She catches Charlotte looking out of the window. 'Have you never been to the highlands?'

'Never had the chance. I'm quite cooped up, to be honest. Security protocols for expats are very tight.'

'That's a shame. It's such a striking landscape.'

'I've seen photos. It looks like the dry Wild West in a way. Like someone could start walking towards the rolling hills on the horizon and just disappear.'

'You should come to Malanje. You might learn a lot about the country, in a way you wouldn't here.'

'I wish. I thought I would travel more with this posting, but it's just Luanda. Ironic, really, to be abroad and see barely anything foreign.' She sighs. 'Wait, is the explosion linked to Jake's case?'

'No, I don't think so. It was after he left Malanje the last time, before now.'

'Could be coincidence, but there is more to Jake than he'd like anyone to know. Take my advice.' Charlotte stands up and looks down at Lena. 'Don't get tangled up with him and his circumstances. I have to deal with him because it's in my job description, but you...' She shuffles her papers together to attempt to put them into a manila folder. 'I presume you have another job to do out here. Don't let him mess that up as well.'

The phone rings at the hotel bedside.

'Lena,' Kojo says, sounding breathless. 'We found you.' He sounds like he's smiling. 'How's Jake?'

'It's a bit of a mess.' She tells him about the embassy visits, the prison conditions, and the plan to convince Jake to sign the agreement never to come back to Angola, and then be done with it. She keeps it factual and businesslike.

'And he'll get out of there safely,' Kojo says. 'Well done, you made sure he was not forgotten. I knew you would.'

'Thanks.' She pauses. She can't remember the last time anyone had such high confidence in her, with just her word as proof.

'Are you needed there much longer?' he asks.

'Is there news about DJ?'

'WFP announced they will be re-starting the Malanje flights tomorrow, unless there are other incidents. Maria's cousin Vaumara in Cuango radioed CWA to say that DJ came to her just after the explosion, but only stayed a few hours that night. Her radio's gone down now, but security permitting, we could go out and meet with her if you'd be prepared to do it. Would you be ready to come back?'

'Of course! That's my whole reason for being here. This is a sideshow, fixing Jake's prison predicament. Get me out of here, will you?'

'We can arrange a ticket to be waiting at the WFP desk at the domestic side of the airport tomorrow morning. You will be on the flight to Malanje, if there is a pilot crazy enough to try it.'

She hangs up the phone and sits back. The hotel room is bare except for a crucifix over the bed and a sole window. The view is obscured by security bars and an air conditioner churning out lukewarm air and mildew.

She hates the feeling of being in limbo, waiting for a chance to be truly useful to somebody. Somebody other than Jake.

Twenty-three

The flights are going. Lena can't fully explain her excitement. She makes a last visit to Jake's cell to explain that she is heading back to the highlands.

'You're leaving me?'

'You'll be fine, Jake.' She speaks too fast but can't seem to slow down. 'The wheels are turning, it just takes some time. But they know you are here, the Angolans won't be able to touch you again. The day after tomorrow you'll be taken by the embassy to the international terminal and away you'll go.'

'What about my story?'

'Jake, it's over. You can get back to the UK and write the best story you can, but your time here is over. My time working on it is over. I need to get back to Malanje, Jake. There are things I have to deal with.'

He won't meet her gaze.

'You have a lot of people pulling for you now,' she says. 'Kojo agreed with Carlos. Now that the embassy's involved, you'll be okay.'

'You trust these people? Carlos Macedo is notorious for playing all sides of the game. And you think Kojo has clean hands?'

'What do you have against Kojo?'

'Lena, how long has he been in Malanje? What's keeping him there? Probably the friendship with Carlos is quite lucrative.'

'You're talking rubbish.'

'Think like a journalist, Lena. Look for what's not said, and you never know what you'll uncover.'

She waves away his accusations. She just needs to deliver on her task and get out of there. 'Whatever, Jake. I am here to tell you that you'll be fine, but I have to go.'

'That's it? You're just going to piss off back to Malanje? Back to Kojo and his cronies?'

'Who the hell do you think you are?' Her impatience to be out of that place rises further. 'You don't know anything about Kojo. He is a truly good person. He's calm and thoughtful, working to help other people. Doesn't leap to conclusions – the total opposite of you.

'You are clever, Jake, I give you that. But you can't read people. You don't take any time to relate or learn from others in the slightest.' She remembers how he treated her back at the villa with such disdain, before she was useful to him. 'You pursue a killer story at all costs. And where does that get you? Nowhere but…' She gestures around her.

He looks at the floor. She can hear him breathing, confined within that cell. His fear of being left alone is palpable.

Guilt blows through her like a sudden unexpected breeze and she stands there with divided feelings. Her weight shifts from foot to foot as she fails to think of a way to make things better.

'Anyway,' she says, 'I have to find DJ.'

He looks up. 'DJ? You know DJ?'

'How do you know DJ?'

He doesn't reply.

'Jake, what aren't you telling me?'

'I met DJ in a bar in Luanda. That DJ can really drink. Anyone – man, woman, old geezer – they were no match. We got talking. About blood diamonds, and everything. They invited me to come and visit them working at a clinic in Luremo.'

'They? Who's they?'

'DJ and Maria. Maria and DJ. Everyone knew them together.'

'What does DJ have to do with your diamonds story?'

'They thought that there was something funny going on with the children in the villages, not showing up for clinic. When there are no doctors to be heard of, the chance to see a nurse would be jumped all over, wouldn't it? But they were going out to these villages, for these scheduled clinics, and there wasn't a child to be seen. The men were off fighting, and the mums and grandmothers, no one was talking.'

Her heart races. She wants him to speed up and get to the point. Instead he slows down to keep her longer.

'Before I was dismissed I had arranged a field visit to Malanje and Luremo. I rang up Maria and planned to stay with them. The embassy didn't know where I was going, that was probably what pissed them off in the end. Conflict zone and unauthorised travel, you know how it is. But I needed to get the last bits of evidence for the story, you see.

'When I got there, it was all different from before. Maria was cold and DJ was shoving me off like a jealous husband. I tried to convince Maria to help me gather info – she would have been brilliant at it. She has all these connections and people would never suspect her. But DJ got a bit aggressive. Started pushing me towards the door, told me I was stirring up trouble.'

She sits down on the bare metal bed. It squeaks in surprise.

She looks down at her hands, turned upwards on her knees. Powerless hands.

'Why do you need to find him?' Jake asks.

'Him, who?'

'DJ, why is he a concern of yours?'

She stares at him. His expression changes as he starts to understand.

'You're his sister, aren't you? I see it in your face now. Don't know why I didn't before.'

'What are you trying to say?'

'What? What did I say wrong?'

'We're family. I'm DJ's sister. She's my sister.' She gets up and starts to pace the cell. She feels trapped. 'For fuck's sake Jake, why did you call her a man?'

'Shit, shit, shit…'

'Why did you call her a man?' she repeats, raising her voice. 'What are you playing at?'

'Sorry, shit, sorry if I messed something up, but DJ was a man. Or passed as one. Married to a beautiful woman. Introduced himself as such. Ask anyone.'

She is going to shout denials but as she examines Jake's shocked face she can tell that he is not lying. Blood rushes to her ears. Her face, her skin and her extremities all burn angry.

'Of course,' he says, gaining his composure. 'It all makes sense now.'

'What the fuck are you saying?'

'She's a dyke. I should've seen it. It's obvious now that you say it. The London look, more appropriate in Camden than here.'

'You're giving advice about how to blend in with the locals? Are you fucking kidding me?'

'Explains everything. The defensiveness of the woman, why she didn't even listen to the logic.'

'She wouldn't serve as your spy, you mean.'

'Even though it could stem the tide of the finances – literally, we could stop the war!'

'You're crazy. "Delusions of grandeur" – does that mean anything to you? Maybe they didn't want to work with you because it's risky to be asking these kinds of questions!'

'It would've been perfect.' Jake looks out of the barred window as if Malanje were just outside.

'You're a fucking idiot. Do you know that Maria was killed? Right after you visited? Who did you talk to when you were out there? Did people see you together?'

Jake shakes his head, won't meet her eye. 'No, no… I was discreet. Absolutely. No one saw us. She's dead? Oh that's really…' He sits down on the bed frame. 'Fuck,' he says.

'Now DJ's gone, you see? Either because she's out of her mind with grief or because someone is threatening her too. And I have to find her. I'm all she's got left.'

'Yes, I see. Poor girl, she more or less blended in but that's because she had Maria.' He pulls at the collar of his shirt as if there is a draught. 'People accepted them, the nice couple, the perfect cover. But now, with Maria gone –' he gives a judgemental sigh – 'they'll close ranks. If she hadn't run, she would have been ejected one way or another. She'll never fit in anywhere again.'

Twenty-four

'Trust me, my child. You'll be fine.'

Lena's legs couldn't stay still. As she sat on the edge of her parents' bed, she kept them swinging so that no one else would see her nervousness. She sat on her hands to hold them tight. All her eight years she had been dreading this moment of going in front of the congregation and having to take communion.

Papa said it was nothing to be worried about, but she didn't really believe him. Mama acted as if it was already decided by destiny.

'DJ never did communion. Why do I have to?' Lena said, trying to stay still long enough for her hair to be plaited.

Mama pressed her chin downwards so that she could give a sharp look from above purple horn-framed glasses. 'You know why. Because it is a commandment from God, to the faithful.' Her face was pulled tight, like it was when she was protecting the girls from danger. 'Your sister has other ideas.'

That wasn't why, though. DJ would never wear this white dress in front of people. Everyone knew that.

But she didn't argue, and Mama softened. She knew Lena would do what was asked. 'DJ will come around. You have to want it. To welcome God's love in your life. And you, my sweet Magdalena, my angel, you have worked for it. You are ready. I know you are.'

She finished the second long black plait and seemed satisfied, patting any imaginary strays into place.

'I have something for you,' Mama said, 'so you will always remember this day.' She moved to her side table and reached into her jewellery box. Lena was rarely allowed to look inside.

Mama opened Lena's palm with one hand and placed the other fist on top. Lena saw the raised veins tracing the ligaments and bone. When Mama lifted her hand away, in Lena's was a gold chain with a flat bronze medal attached. She moved it closer to her eye and saw it was the portrait of an older man carrying a child on his shoulders. He had a staff like in biblical times and he was smiling. It smelled of old metal.

'St Christopher,' Mama said. 'Protecting children, protecting travellers. As he protected Christ. See here.' She turned over the medal to let Lena see both sides. 'God looks after the faithful.'

It was beautiful, she didn't have to lie to say so. But as Mama fastened it around her neck, it had the feeling of something that didn't quite fit.

Mama turned her to look in the mirror. Perfectly symmetrical plaits reached down past her shoulder blades and seemed to meet with Mama's approval. 'It's for your protection,' she said, patting with both hands. 'When Papa and I cannot be near you.'

She looked at her reflection. She wanted to see a resemblance to her mother – the beautiful round red lips, the blonde wavy hair. But the girl peering back at her looked like no one in particular, not Mama, nor Papa. She had Papa's dark eyes and complexion, but she had always wanted more of a recognisable connection with somebody. She looked somewhat like DJ, she had to admit. However, the anger that usually masked her sister's face distorted it and set her apart. No, DJ didn't want to look like a girl. Lena was alone.

'All God asks is that you keep your heart open to Him,' Mama continued, kissing her on the top of her head. 'And when the time comes, when He asks it of you, you make an effort. He will know that you are trying, and He will be there for you when you need Him.'

She nodded, thinking about the moments ahead in front of the priest and everyone they knew. She fingered the medal that lay on her chest, so light she could barely feel it hanging. She knew she had no choice but to wear it, always.

Twenty-five

You remember him well. The blond FCO man. He was clever, you'll give him that. Clever enough to piece together disparate information to find a pattern no one else could see. But something about him you guarded against, instinctively. He was too sure of himself, would make a serious mistake at some point.

Maria, wonderful, foolish woman, she liked the man. God knows why. She trusted nearly everyone, at first. With Maria it took a long time for someone to fall in her esteem. She had a basic love for people, proved to be undeserved in a small number of cases.

What did she see in him? Couldn't she realise that he was all artifice and arrogance? You remember how she lingered over the last beer, leaning in to hear more about his theories. How she seemed to forget you were there, when he talked and went on and on. Ignored your pleas to turn in early.

What did he tell her that night? You should have stayed, served as a filter for his diplomat-speak. Should have contradicted his assumptions and translated them back into common sense. You should have made her see how he failed to read the situation, got all the local politics twisted the wrong way round. To a man like him, the unspoken agreements and protections would always remain a mystery.

The memories bring pain to your chest, your shoulders, your scalp. As if your skin wants to contract to prevent you from falling further to pieces.

Even as you loved Maria, you wished then and wish now so badly that she hadn't trusted so much. It was Maria who invited him to stay in Malanje. It seemed like it was an intellectual exercise for him; he wanted to prove his theories right. Maria, as a woman with many brothers, thought she understood men. She knew that he had something to prove. Even if he knew nobody in that conflict-scarred town, some honour was at stake.

But she wasn't naïve. She realised her mistakes, tried to fix them. The timing wasn't right for his visit. UNITA and MPLA would both know about his investigations. And they would link her to his inquiry, even if she had said no, and broken off the interaction.

And she tried to protect you, that's what kills you. Tried to keep it away from you, the whispers in Kikongo, which she knew you didn't understand. The animal skull left on the threshold, the day before the explosion. She tried to explain away your feeling of foreboding.

'Why didn't she tell me?' you cry, over and over again. You no longer know if you are screaming out loud or in your nightmares.

You have a fever which takes hold and won't let go. Sisters come into your room at intervals to take your temperature and give injections. They plead with you to drink some water and try to keep food down.

You are tortured by memories, ones that are getting more sinister and twisted as the days pass. Moments that once were beautiful now feel ominous and telling. Everything could have been different, if only you had read the signs. If only Maria's trust in you had been stronger, she would have been less vulnerable to others.

If only.

Oh God, Jesus Mary mother of God, you see Maria looking down at her blackened self. You feel her intense pain, the clothing drenched from the blood. You watch her turn away from you, looking up at the ceiling.

You remember how she closed her eyes, and then she whispered: 'I'm not going to make it, am I?' You don't know if she was talking to you, or asking God for an answer.

Twenty-six

What do I do? Lena sinks to her knees next to the ratty hotel bed. The bedspread is rough and smells of insecticide.

She thinks back to the moments of her life when decisions were made. The choices were never made by her. Dad's café closing after his stroke. Mum's funeral – all the details arranged by the church committee. DJ's postings abroad. Never consulted about any of it.

She's not surprised to hear about DJ and Maria. She knew that DJ was not conventional, suspected as much about her sexuality. There were signs of it when she still lived at home, the other children saw it too. Nothing shocking about that.

But to go so far as to live as someone else, or a version of yourself that is something else? That severs a thread that connects you to your past self. It is a much more profound choice. It makes a gap of continuity, leaving few leads to follow. And when there are threats against you, against your family and those you love, surely you need some continuity?

She feels herself shake. Her foundation is crumbling. What else is changed? What else has she got wrong?

*

DJ, why didn't you tell me?

I would have understood. You know I would have.

You can trust me, DJ. I'm not a child. I know love comes differently for different people. I've had a few lovers myself, ones you've never heard anything about. You never asked.

Why don't we ever talk? We haven't spoken since Mum's funeral.

DJ, I need to find you.

We need to talk. Really talk. We used to talk.

Are you okay? Tell me that you are okay.

How the hell am I going to find you?

No answer.

She recalls words she memorised long ago, at the urging of her mother. She didn't want to do it, hated being up there at the centre of attention. But she learned it anyway, of course she did. Mum's beliefs were forceful.

Her hand goes to the necklace that she still wears, never takes it off.

Divine Host, I adore Thee, she remembers. *With the angels who fill the sanctuary and hover over the tabernacle, the same way they hovered over the cave of Bethlehem in the Holy Night.*

She wonders about these angels – do they still hover? Can the angels and the saints provide the protection that was promised?

She remembers looking at the stone altar of St Francis's in Stockwell, dim in the winter light, candles warm all around. Do the saints remain with the believers who go to church, or can they be with anyone anywhere? If you wear the ornaments, do the rituals?

I adore Thee, my God, with the Blessed Virgin, and in union with all the saints.

Mary, Mother of God.

She finds her hands in prayer.

Mother, Mum, what do I do?

Mum, Mama, are you there? Are you listening? What am I supposed to do? What if Maria's death wasn't an accident? What if Jake caused it somehow, with trying to recruit her to report for his blood diamonds story? And I've been focusing my time on helping him, when that's what hurt DJ? Ripped her life apart, killed the love of her life.

Mama, you always used to hold steady. Even as DJ erupted, as she did so often, you usually maintained your poise, although you could argue back as hard as she did. But you and Dad saw past her impulsive ways and understood. I didn't, was too young to get it.

Can you see DJ? Is she okay?

Does she know I am trying to find her?

Mama, Mum, if you are listening, if there's any help you can give me, give me a sign.

Any direction, any consolation in this God forsaken place.

Please Mama.

Please.

I do believe, Lord.

Help my belief, increase my faith.

The air conditioner shakes itself on, spitting out more stale air. It makes her shudder, then chide herself for being pathetic.

She drops her hands into her lap.

She feels utterly overwhelmed with emotions. But it is unclear whether these come solely from inside her, or whether she's absorbed a myriad of other people's experiences through the stories of the past few days.

After a few minutes, she brings herself up off her knees, slouches onto the bed and sighs.

For distraction, she turns on the radio.

Savimbi está morto. Repito, Savimbi foi morto. O MPLA relata que as 6.00 desta manhã o líder rebelde foi baleado, morrendo quase instantaneamente.

The UNITA rebel leader Jonas Savimbi has been shot and killed. Shot fifteen times in the head, back and chest by MPLA soldiers. Even a survivor like him cannot escape mortality when the time has come.

Part III

Twenty-seven

You hear the kitchen radio breaking the silence. You know the news must be significant or else it never would have been allowed to echo through the halls like this.

You feel dizzy as you walk through the swinging door into the kitchen. Your fever has lifted, leaving you quiet and calm inside. The agitated despair has settled into a heavy sadness. It sits on your lungs and makes any fast movements difficult.

The kitchen is large, whitewashed, and full of preparations for the communal evening meal. The large pot of cassava bubbles away but everything else is still. Sister Therese is there, her hand frozen above the basket of multicoloured beans she is sorting. Mama Iglese leans her bulk on the dining table and blows her cheeks out round with the impact of the words spoken through the speakers:

Savimbi está morto. Repito, Savimbi foi morto. O MPLA relata que as 6.00 desta manhã o líder rebelde foi baleado, morrendo quase instantaneamente.

Savimbi has been shot and killed. Twenty-six years of fighting – finished in an instant.

You stumble and fall into a wooden chair. No one looks at you. No one makes eye contact with anyone else. Eyes are glazed, looking outward, while minds focus inward. People allow themselves to dive into their memories, their terrors, their hopes, and the uncertain future.

Your life's work has revolved around this war. Now it is over. You feel as if you should be celebrating. Instead it's like another crucial piece of the puzzle that is your identity, this piece too has dropped out.

There is no longer any chance to be whole. First you lost Maria, now you've lost your purpose.

There is nothing left to do but disappear, like water into the cracked earth.

Twenty-eight

Kojo, Jeanette and Brad suspend their conversation as the morning radio repeats the statement they never imagined they would hear:

Savimbi está morto. UNITA concordou em um cessar-fogo incondicional. O governo pediu à calma.

Savimbi is dead. UNITA has agreed an unconditional ceasefire. The government appeals for calm. These words are repeated without any more information.

'What the hell?' Brad finally spits out, then starts laughing.

Jeanette blinks, looking from Kojo to Brad, unbelieving. 'The war, it's over? It's bloody finished?' She starts jumping up and down and clapping her hands. 'It's bloody finished!'

'It's over, it's fucking well finished!' Brad jumps up as well and holds both of her hands in his.

Kojo remains sitting and silent. The war over. So sudden. Why had he not seen this coming? It is all going to move in a rush now and he just needs a bit of time. To think through the new scenarios that he had never considered.

'It is great news, great, if it is true...' he says. His friends – his closest friends, closer than others he's known for a lifetime – are giddy and dancing around the small shared kitchen.

Will the ceasefire hold? There are millions of soldiers and civilians with UNITA. Do they know the news in the bush? Where will they go when there's nothing more to fight for?

Brad is singing John Lennon's 'War is Over' while dancing Jeanette in circles. She laughs loudly, a woman loving the attention.

Kojo sees what he hadn't seen earlier: they are lovers. Of course. He was too focused on the work to see. He feels a throb of envy – why is it that they find love and it did not work out for him? – but he quickly sets the thoughts back in their place.

'The two of you,' he says, 'you are together?'

Jeanette drops Brad's hands, but it is too late to deny it. 'Yes, darling. You know me, I don't usually get attached. But this guy,' she gestures to Brad, who is grinning and dancing a little jig on the spot, 'this one might be different.'

'But we won't let it interfere with the job, you know,' Brad adds. 'Never would.'

'Ah, well, you're grown ups, aren't you?' He looks away as he feels Jeanette examining his face. She probably knows him better than any other woman, after everything they've been through as a team. Does she know about Maria, that short time so long ago? He doesn't tell her about the inclinations of his heart, but she probably has intuition. She's never said anything, never seen him openly take a chance with anyone since. She helps him keep up the pretence of the confident leader. He appreciates that. She can't know he is in pieces at times. Fragments that have no one to come together for.

But he can't dwell on that for long. He starts to think through what will happen as the news of Savimbi's death gets out. If the ceasefire holds, if there are no setbacks or splinter

138

groups… And if the numbers are right, and 3.8 million people are indeed displaced by this war, then millions of UNITA supporters will be coming out of the bush. They will be on the move now, or very soon.

'People,' he says, standing up. 'I share your excitement, but we have work to do. Huge volumes of work, once these people hear the news and start to move. I'm going to radio WFP.'

Twenty-nine

Lena isn't surprised to see that the pilot is the same one that flew her out to Malanje the first time. The lanky walk, as if his legs are longer than he expected. The dark glasses and lack of engagement with others, except the bare minimum.

It's a privilege, seeing Angola from the air. The perspective that comes with altitude gives you a glimpse of the stark dry beauty of this country. Once outside the reach of the city, the landscape blends colours together like a painting.

DJ, I'm coming back. Hang on, I'm coming. Wait for me, please wait.

The pilot announces that the landing has changed. Now they can descend in a straight line. There is no need to spiral as supposedly there are no more surface-to-air missiles aimed to take it down. UNITA has stepped back; with no Savimbi, there is no leader to dictate their movements.

The machine twists slightly left and right to try to aim for the dirt line in the dust ahead.

'It will be sharp!' the pilot shouts over the noise of the engines and the wind resistance. 'The runway's not that long!'

Lena braces against the seat in front of her, and wishes her seatbelt was more than just a thin piece of grey nylon. She holds her breath.

With a sharp bang, the plane hits the ground and bounces twice. The engines roar into reverse. There are a few moments while the plane continues to rattle ahead at speed. She anticipates an impact and holds her breath.

Defying expectations again, the plane slows down to a bumpy canter. The passengers around her straighten up, smooth their hair, and don't meet each other's eye. That way they can pretend they weren't scared.

The air turns quiet again as the villa's generator whirs to a finish. Lena feels her shoulders relax down without the steady din. Amazing how loud it is when the generator is on. It crowds the mind. Thoughts get shaken and broken up, come out as fragments.

She and Kojo are sitting side by side on the front veranda of the villa. They should be inside due to the threat of mosquitos or worse, but they both linger. They look out, not at each other. She smells his scent – a slight hint of an unfamiliar aftershave, mixed with a clean-shirt smell. She is excited to be back there with him and the team, doesn't really understand all the reasons why. She still feels a bit awkward though, as the one with the least experience.

A dog howls in the dark, urging others to join in.

'Wonder what he's so upset about,' she says.

'Worries he can't tell anybody else?' he offers.

'So he has to howl? Disturbing our ears?'

'Maybe he thinks it sounds like music. Like Fado, singing out your pain.'

'You're an authority on Portuguese music now?' Her voice sounds harsher than she wants it to.

He doesn't say anything.

After more stillness, with the sounds of animals and cars in the distance, she has to speak up.

'He tried to recruit Maria, you know.'

'The dog?'

'Ha ha, very funny. No – Jake.'

'For the FCO?'

'No, for his own personal thing. "Project Blood Diamonds Investigation". He was hoping for a front-page story.'

'He didn't succeed, though.'

'No, she refused. Apparently, DJ got pretty angry, felt threatened by it. Jake thought she was a man.'

'I see.'

'You're not surprised.'

He takes a moment. 'No.'

'Does everyone here know something about my sister I don't know? Why didn't anyone fucking tell me that she was going around as a man?'

He opens his mouth as if to argue but then pulls it shut.

'You must think I was so stupid that I didn't see it,' she says.

He chooses his words slowly. 'Not stupid. Never stupid.'

'I'm not a child. You people, you think you're so much more experienced than I am? Well I might not know Angola, but you don't know everything there is to know about DJ and me.'

'It wasn't respectful; I'm sorry.'

She feels so angry she could shout and kick, but she very much wants to keep emotions under control. She's got a job to do here, wants to carry it off like a professional. She'll show them.

'Look, Lena,' he starts to say more, but seems to lose his way. 'I… I was trying… to protect DJ.'

'Protect her, well that plan fucking failed spectacularly, didn't it?'

'Protect, or – no, that's not right. Respect them, DJ and Maria. Respect their wishes. It was what they wanted.'

'Whatever,' she cuts him off. 'It's done now. Just makes me so angry that we lost time. For fuck's sake.'

He looks out past the hedges and fencing surrounding the villa, at the stars appearing.

'What if someone overheard Jake, or was watching him? Thought Maria and DJ were part of it?'

'Maria had such deep connections in this part of the country... no one would believe it of her.'

'You think so?'

'I am sure of it. That was her protection.'

'What if, I don't know, someone bore a grudge against her, against them? For their lifestyle?'

'What makes you say that?'

'Could happen.'

'That's the thing though. You need to get to know Angola. Some things you'd think they would be strict about, they are quite relaxed. Like women living together. Children out of wedlock, mixed race couples. Things are less rigid at the margins, because the centre has been blown away.'

'Then why didn't they live openly, if it was so relaxed?'

'Well, it's still a traditional, rural place. People accepted them together, but I think it was much easier for everyone if it was that way. They lived as a nice normal couple.'

'But you said machismo is very strong. Couldn't someone have been jealous of them? Infatuated with Maria maybe, and aiming to get rid of DJ, getting the wrong target?'

'It is possible, I suppose. I don't like to think of people that way.' He looks down at his hands as their shoulders just fail to touch. 'I don't have much time to think about relationships.'

After a minute, he says, 'I'm sorry if we held back on you. We should have said something when you first arrived.'

'Yeah, that would've been better.' She tries to take some of the sarcasm out of her voice. She doesn't know why, but she wants to earn his respect. She very much wants him to like her, to think her opinions are worth something. Him and the whole team, of course. That matters, for some reason.

'Are there other relationships going on,' she asks, 'between staff members?'

'Well, you know about Jeanette and Brad, do you?'

She raises her eyebrows but she's not surprised. She thought as much.

'Women have an instinct about these things, I suppose. Me, I don't notice unless it is obvious. With the local team, there is not much gossip there. Many of them are married already from a young age.'

'Really?'

'Younger than you, even.' He smiles at her. 'And me, I'm ancient.' He rubs his hand over his bald head, as if he's self-conscious. 'What about you?' he asks. 'Do you have anybody special back in London?'

She pauses, too long. 'Yes, I'm living with him actually. Long-term thing. Known him since we were kids.'

'He doesn't mind you being out here in a war zone?'

'Didn't like the idea, but he knows I have to do what I can to find DJ.'

'What's his name?'

'Lucien. He's always been there for me, you know?'

He nods as if he might know how that feels.

'What about you? Do you have anyone here, or back in Ghana?'

He shakes his head. 'I did, once. Long time ago now.'

The dog howls out again and she feels sorry for Kojo. It seems like he has held onto an emptiness for quite some time.

She changes the subject. 'When can we get to Cuango, to talk to Maria's cousin?'

His tone changes back from the personal to the professional. 'This ceasefire is so new that security is quite unpredictable... It could be a free-for-all, as various armed groups have different ideas of what surrender is. It might be quite touch and go. There are command-and-control issues on each side, although I have to say UNITA's discipline has been harsh enough to keep people obedient for a long time.'

He gets up and brushes dust off his trousers. 'But security permitting, I think we can borrow a motorbike and go to Cuango tomorrow.' His eyes connect with hers, to see if that's what she wants to hear. 'It'll be an early one then, leaving just after 6 am. We should get some sleep.' He swings open the screen door and is gone without looking back.

She hears the snap of the door shut and is left with the noises of dogs and insects. Why did she say that about Lucien? That was stupid. There was no need to bring him into things. She pads back inside quickly, shutting her bedroom door against all outsiders.

It is a leap of faith, letting someone else steer. It's the logical choice, she knows – he can read the roads and the changes in the landscape; she needs to learn. But she doesn't like to depend on him, especially not now. She resists the need to hold her arms around his waist. She should trust him. But she has other feelings too, and doesn't know what to do with those.

'The road seems clear,' Kojo shouts back over his shoulder. 'We should be okay until the police outpost.'

She nods, even though she knows he can't look back and see her face. But perhaps he can feel her movements, in his back.

The air is hot, even in the shade. Feels like a hairdryer is blowing at them, hampering their progress. He must feel it too, as he revs the engine louder.

The road is shaded by trees that are linked above with lianas laced together. The sunlight flashes in and out in a haphazard pattern; it makes her blink and refocus at every change. The red dust makes a taste in her mouth that she knows she won't be able to lose.

Before they set off, Kojo said that anyone on a motorcycle has to constantly look for indications of landmines – the biggest danger on these roads. Any sign of recent digging, upset earth, or lines under the dirt could be a mine or a trigger for an improvised explosive.

She is vigilant and scans the road every moment. She wants to be efficient and effective, defending against any threat.

Can't let anything happen to her. Kojo's mind moves in this repetitive refrain as he steers the bike. DJ would never forgive him a second time.

There is something exhilarating about having to pay attention to every movement. Weighing every observation in a split second for its significance, making the quick adjustments. It blocks out all extraneous, unnecessary thoughts.

He hasn't told her the whole truth; it gnaws at his mind. But it will all work out in the end, surely.

Up ahead there is a collection of houses. 'That's Remo,' he calls out. 'A good place to stop for water.'

When the bike comes to a halt she takes off her helmet. 'How far is it to Cuango?'

'If the road stays clear, not long now. Another hour and we'll get there.'

He looks at her. She has a line across her forehead from the helmet. Trails of dust have turned muddy from sweat down her jaw. But she is still striking. Can't see it herself, doesn't hold herself like someone who knows it. But she is.

'At Cuango, the road forks,' he continues. 'One way is very quiet, leads up to a Catholic nunnery. The other way leads to Luremo Sul.'

'Where Maria's family was from?'

He nods. He wonders if Lena remembers Okea's story some days back. She has heard so many stories and destinations, it would not necessarily stand out.

To Lena, Cuango doesn't look like much, but it does seem to be a place of slightly elevated importance, this village around a dusty road junction. There are more concrete foundations to the buildings, a few cars. A solitary street sign announces twenty kilometres to the Congolese border.

It is deserted. There's no sign of Maria's cousin. Knocking on her door is met with silence. There is no one to ask, no animals even to show any evidence of life. Just shacks along the road, with broken windows and smashed fencing.

'I was worried about this,' he says. 'I should have been more concerned when Vaumara wasn't there to confirm yesterday.' His eyes search the horizon. 'I had heard UNITA forced people along this corridor to march towards the border. But I thought this place would have been protected, because of the MPLA police outpost.'

'Everyone's gone? On a forced march?'

'All who had not managed to escape before their arrival,' he says grimly. 'Who knows where they are now?'

'Probably waiting for us in the camps that are growing more populated by the minute.'

'You're starting to think like a humanitarian, Lena. DJ would be proud.'

She looks at him, wondering if he is being ironic. Probably not.

He frowns, mulling things over.

'Where's the police outpost?' she asks.

'It's the last building on the left before the turn.'

Her hopes of seeing anyone dissolve as she sees that it lies abandoned as well.

'I'm surprised Carlos didn't say anything,' he says. 'All these northern provinces are in his patch.'

She turns to look at him. Jake had used the word 'lucrative' to describe friendships with Carlos. How close are the two men, really? What's in it for Kojo? There must be something, some kind of two-way street. 'How much do you really trust that guy?' she says.

'You have to trust some people, Lena, or else you'll never get anywhere.'

'But we've come this way for nothing?' she says, kicking at the ground.

'Sorry, looks like that.'

'Can't we go further? To Luremo?'

'Security didn't clear us for further on. We'll have to return to base and radio in for clearance.'

'Fucking hell!' she shouts, knowing no one can hear but him. She wants to reach out and hit something. Hit him, shake him. 'What am I doing here, Kojo? It's like all I do is stall and stumble when I need to move!' She spins in the dust and marches away, swinging her arms as if she's trying to swat a circling fly. He lets her go down the street without argument.

The sun burns with no shade above. It is too beastly hot to rage against the inevitable. It is futile and she is drained.

She comes back to him after a few minutes. But she hasn't managed to work out how to explain herself or say sorry for the outburst.

'Fine,' she says. 'Let's radio security about these roads and try to get out further as soon as possible, okay?'

He nods but holds up a hand. 'Lena, there is a bigger picture. I need to take the team back to Quessa tomorrow for a huge delivery. There are thousands of new arrivals in bad shape. I want to find DJ just as much as you, but there are other people here with urgent needs.'

'Do you really think you want to find DJ as much as I do? That's quite a presumption. She's not your sister.'

His face falls. 'You're right, of course. I shouldn't have said that.'

She feels a burning mix of emotions. Anger and frustration fight against embarrassment and attraction. Anger wins, but the others linger.

Thirty

Jeanette is out of breath as she briefs Lena about their work in the camps since Savimbi's death. She seems conflicted, as if they were found on the back foot and now need to make up for it in concentrated effort. There are serious concerns for the 1.5 million people displaced in Malanje province who may soon be on the move. These people – ex-soldiers, child conscripts, women, orphans – have all been living behind UNITA's wall of harsh discipline and no communication. No vaccinations. No sanitation. No education.

'No idea what to expect,' Jeanette says. 'But our work is only going to grow exponentially.'

Lena tries to keep her mind on the numbers and tasks, but she keeps going back to questions around Vaumara, Okea and the minefield, Fernanda and her lost sister. What's happened to them? Are they marching through dangerous areas trying to reach lost loved ones? Are they under fire? Are the children okay? Is anyone safe now?

'And no one knows UNITA's moves at this point,' Jeanette continues. 'They seem to be letting people go, but you could always get a rogue commander who prefers to be king of his own domain. They punish people for coming out of the bush, take aid workers hostage, that kind of thing. This place has a history of spontaneous massacres, so watch out.'

Lena blinks away images of a firing squad, the faces of the victims hidden by blindfolds. Could that happen to DJ? She shudders and shakes her head, knocking her imagination back to focus on the present.

'What can I do to help?' she asks.

'We hoped you'd say that,' Jeanette replies.

In the car on the way back to Quessa, Lena sees the checkpoints: abandoned. Where did they all go? The boys with the guns, the leaders hiding behind sunglasses? The Land Rover drives over an old chain in the dust.

Tents, boxes, and small constructions using scraps of fabric line the road in the miles outside the camp's borders. As they move past, it becomes clear that these are makeshift homes, providing scant shade and little protection from the elements. Some feeling of security must come from having something over your head. Even if it's so flimsy as to be translucent, it still could be better than the open sky.

As the car speeds forward, she catches a glimpse of a pair of children, one older than the other, clinging to each other under a patterned blue cloth tied to three sticks. The fear and surprise on their faces – at the noise of the car, or the white face looking out of the window – are caught in the moment like a photograph. She twists in her seat to keep her eyes on their little shelter, shrinking in the distance. Is that all the protection they have? Isn't anyone looking after them?

Turning forward again, she sees that these kinds of shelters dot up the hillsides, block the paths, fall into the sewer ditches, and clog the arteries of an already overflowing camp. My God, she thinks. There's thousands upon thousands of them.

The Land Rover pulls in towards the clinic and people look up slowly, as if dazed. Sebastião navigates carefully to avoid the people on foot or crouching at the roadside. He steers around the stray dogs and a crutch lying in the road.

Before opening her door, she surveys the faces through the window. A little boy stares at her, open-mouthed. He wears only an oversized t-shirt, grey with dirt, the neck stretched so wide it is off one bony shoulder. The t-shirt is ripped through with chains of small holes, barely holding together, and his skinny frame shows through the gaps. Before she can say anything, the boy snaps his mouth shut and frowns. He pushes away from the car, back into the mass of bodies.

The crowd presses forward, with occasional strips of brighter-coloured clothes standing out from an otherwise ragged, monotone bulk of people in bad shape. The children have lost hair in clumps. They cling to the hip of a mother or onto the back of an elder sibling. They don't smile. She has never seen people look so tough and so vulnerable at the same moment. Just the fact that they have arrived in the camp shows some extreme personal power of endurance.

'Ah Christ,' Jeanette says, to no one in particular.

'I'll sort out the water bladders ASAP,' Brad says, opening his door and landing with a bounce.

Kojo looks back at her. 'Are you ready for this?' he asks.

'Ready as I'll ever be.' She opens her door carefully, concerned not to knock anyone over. They move to allow the door to open and watch her movements. Many of them have yellow or bloodshot eyes. Sickness is already taking hold.

A woman dressed in bright yellow cloth straightens up tall and lifts her voice to shout in a language Lena doesn't understand. Other women's voices rise up in a call and response that raises pitch. Lena strains to piece together the meaning but can't decipher it. Men hit their walking sticks and crutches on the ground in a gathering rhythm. People surround the Land Rover, Sebastião still inside, and bang on the metal. They are angry about something, getting to the edge of desperate. The children stamp their feet and clap in rhythm, looking up at the adult faces waiting for something to happen.

DJ would know what they are saying, she thinks. She was always good with languages. She should be here instead of me.

Kojo and Jeanette move to the front of the crowd, raising their hands for calm. The shouts and stamping settle into an unhappy murmur. The message passes through the crowd that Jeanette will be opening the clinic. Other local CWA workers explain more detail in the local language, which seems to be better understood. People surge forward towards the clinic doors.

'Lena, over here!' Jeanette calls, as she hastily sets up a table outside her clinic-hut. 'I need you to take down people's names, condition, and village, if at all possible – some kind of identification.'

'Excuse me, sorry, *desculpe-me, por favor...*' She steps over people's feet and around toddlers sitting in the dust. She notices the cracked heels, the misshapen toes, the ring of something like a parasite embedded in a child's scalp. There is no chair. She kneels next to the table and takes out her notebook.

'*Os casos mais urgentes, por favor.*' Jeanette appeals for calm and tries to get those who are in most urgent need of assistance to come forward. '*Mais urgente. De extrema urgência.*'

'*De extrema urgência...*' The murmur runs through the crowd. They shuffle and separate to allow some to pass forward.

Lena takes down the names and details of people coming forward. *Problemas respiratórios, ferimento na cabeça, diarréia, infeccões...* Through gestures and observations she can more

153

or less document the afflictions. She starts to make a list with names of people with more urgent concerns gathering near the top.

A heavily pregnant woman steps forward, holding her back. She speaks in halting Portuguese, and says her name is Avelina. She is very thin, with her cheekbones, collarbone, knees and elbows all jutting out awkwardly, in contradiction to the round belly. She is supported by several women behind her, and a young boy clings to her leg, unheeded, naked except for a beaded necklace. Avelina keeps her eyes closed, breathing hard and sweating.

The woman closest behind her introduces herself as a cousin, Lucia, steering her softly by the shoulders. Lucia explains in Portuguese that Avelina's labour has been long and is giving her terrible back pains, and the baby is not coming out.

Jeanette comes and puts her arm around the pregnant woman, gently steering her into the clinic with Lucia. Her boy starts to protest, held back then soothed by another woman who sweeps him onto her back to hold him still.

Jeanette looks back at the table and crowd and says, 'Girls, get me some disinfectant and sheets, quick.' A local CWA worker named Nuria scurries off with a worried look on her face. The queue of people waiting at the table collectively pauses, their needs suspended for a moment.

Lena doesn't know what to do; should she still take names, or try to help Jeanette? Her pen feels inadequate.

A few minutes later, screams come from inside the clinic, making Lena shrink into her shoulders. She gestures to the person at the front of the queue to wait a moment, and dashes to the door of the clinic.

Knocking at the door, she says, 'Jeanette, can I help?'

'Lena, it's eclampsia. And the baby's back-to-back. I think it's too much for you.'

Nuria pushes the door open, bringing the supplies, and Lena sees Avelina sitting on a tarp on the floor, breathing heavily. Lucia crouches next to her, supporting her cousin from behind and rubbing her back.

'*O bebê precisa sair, que Deus nos ajude.*' Lucia's hands move in smooth circles.

Yes, God please lend us some help, Lena thinks. We'll need it.

Jeanette looks up from her preparations for an instant. 'Ever been at a birth before?'

She shakes her head.

'How are you about blood? Not a fainter, are you?'

'My mum was a midwife.'

'Then you'll be a natural.' Jeanette flicks the needle before putting an IV into the woman's arm. 'Hold this tube up.'

Lena offers her other hand to Avelina, who takes hold.

'*O bebê está a vir,*' Lena says. '*Ele vai ficar bem. Vais conseguir.*' The baby is coming, it will be fine. Avelina nods, eyes closed. Lena quietly repeats the words. She can't think of anything else.

'Back to back is tough, particularly in her state,' Jeanette explains. 'And she's been in labour for a couple of days now, waters broken with a risk of infection.'

Avelina's face strains as her breathing comes to a crescendo. She grips Lucia and Lena's supporting hands on either side with a powerful hold. It looks as if she has lost all layers of fat, leaving behind only skin over closed eyes, muscle and skull. She is taut and determined.

'Put on these gloves,' Jeanette says. 'Maria was trying to trial something for HIV testing to prevent mother-to-infant transmission, but we have no time for the test.' She keeps moving, checking blood pressure and getting forceps and sterilised razor ready. 'We'll need to assist this baby.'

After the IV bag has gone empty and flat, Lena drops the line and holds Avelina's hand with both her own. In between contractions Lucia rubs circles over Avelina's round belly while murmuring gentle words, trying to coax the baby out.

The next hour passes in a rush. Lena is acutely aware of the screams, the salty-thick smell of blood, the tense grip of her two hands. Her legs are cramping.

There is one long scream-groan from Avelina, from deep inside, like an animal trying to wrench loose. The baby emerges, along with a growing circle of red spreading across the floor.

'That's my girl, you're doing it. Come on, you can do it.' Jeanette looks up from where she is delivering the baby with a worried look on her face. '*Bebê está aqui...* the baby is here; hang on, Avelina, you'll see this baby yet.'

Avelina's face is grey and she does not open her eyes.

Lena leans closer to Avelina's ear. '*Bebê está aqui.* Avelina. *Olha, olha para o teu filho.* Please open your eyes, please, *por favor.* Please look at this baby.'

A newborn cry breaks the air. Lena and Lucia laugh at the same instant. Lucia reaches one hand to Lena's shoulder in a moment of relief.

Jeanette swiftly cuts the cord, ties it then performs her checks on the baby and seems satisfied. 'It's healthy, a healthy girl.' She wraps the child in a cloth. 'Lucia,' she says, 'quick, take the child.'

Lucia leaves Avelina's side and reaches for the baby. She wraps her arms around the bundle and murmurs to soothe the cries.

Jeanette wipes her brow with the back of her forearm, leaving sweat and blood in a diluted smear across her forehead.

She speaks quickly to Lena, with no chance for breath. 'We're losing her. She's got to pass the placenta. We need her conscious. I'm going to stich her up as fast as I can, but she's haemorrhaging. Keep talking to her. Keep her awake. Say anything.'

Lena keeps repeating the words from before: '*Bebê está aqui, abra seus olhos, por favor* Avelina.' She pulses her grip on Avelina's hand, trying to think of something else. '*A bebê é uma menina, linda como a sua mãe.*' The baby is a girl, beautiful like her mother. '*Por favor* Avelina, stay awake. Stay with us.'

What would Mum have said at a moment like this? Always so calm and clear-minded in a crisis. Why did she never try to understand Mum's work? Never actually saw her in her element. Now she is useless. Worse than useless. Tongue-tied as this woman slips away.

'Very faint pulse,' Jeanette says. 'Breathing's shallow.'

Avelina's grip grows slack. 'Isn't there something?' Lena asks.

'No transfusions here, I'm afraid. We could try another IV to add volume to her blood, but that would only help a bit. She has to pull herself through.' Jeanette looks for a moment as if she will cry. But then her face hardens.

Lucia sways in the far corner of the clinic, singing to the baby. If she understands what is being said, she shows no sign.

Thirty-one

Avelina's body is taken away by her family, many of them weeping gently as they carry her from the clinic. Lucia ties the baby to her chest with a faded cloth and then helps to carry her cousin. The family does not acknowledge Lena or Jeanette in their grief.

Jeanette squeezes her shoulders as the door swings shut. 'It's terrible,' she says. 'But it happens, too often in this place.' Then she changes her mood like a switch. 'But there are loads of patients out there,' she says. 'I'll need to clean this up, and then we'll try to help more people, okay?'

Lena nods, not convinced.

'Here, have a drink first, child,' Jeanette says, handing her a bottle of water. Lena accepts it without a word. She walks back outside, taking her place again at the table.

She doesn't say much the rest of the day. She writes down people's names and their ailments. She steers the most urgent cases to Jeanette. She forgets to eat or drink as the list grows. A numb feeling takes over her body and mind.

*

The team works past sunset, then darkness falls. Protocols and curfew have been forgotten, as there is too much work to do to plan properly.

The team descends on Jeanette's clinic after nightfall. Some patients remain outside in quiet huddles, looking up each time the clinic door opens. Others have gone back to wherever they will spend the night: huts, tents, rickety shelters, or exposed to the elements. The smells from cooking fires rise up from the haphazard paths. The heat of the day has evaporated, leaving Lena shivery.

Jeanette locks up her most valuable supplies for the night. 'We forgot to have lunch. Or dinner.'

'Or to leave on time for curfew,' Brad says.

Kojo refuses to make eye contact. 'I should have anticipated this. Planned better.' He descends into his own thoughts.

Brad looks around the clinic to see if there is anything to eat. Jeanette bats his hand away from the shelf with the nutritional supplements. Then he finds a chocolate bar in the cabinet and grins. 'I can split it four ways.'

Jeanette takes a square. Kojo shakes his head. Lena nods but is then unsure. Her mouth is too dry.

'Go on, give it a try,' Brad says. 'Or lose your chance!'

Lena takes a bite. She forces her jaw to chew it and rake it down her throat. It burns and her stomach makes a noise she's sure everybody can hear. She runs to the door and vomits outside.

'Tough day,' she hears Jeanette say. 'We didn't prepare her very well, did we?'

They sleep on woven mats on the floor of the clinic. Some clean sheets are folded up to act as pillows, save one that lies on top.

Brad falls asleep instantly, descending into snores. Jeanette giggles. 'Lucky sod,' she whispers. 'Always can sleep at a moment's notice. But that roar!' She gives him a swift elbow to the ribs, which prompts him to roll over, and it drops to a more tolerable level.

'I've had a lot of lovers,' Jeanette says, 'but he is the loudest.' Getting no response from Lena, she continues. 'It's quite natural to think about sex after there's been a death, you know. Connects us to something primal, about life and rebirth, that's what I figure.'

She rolls onto her side to look at Lena. 'Carlos was the quietest. Well, he was a gentleman. Almost never stayed over.'

Lena doesn't react, but Jeanette keeps going. 'You met Carlos, didn't you? Thing is, I knew him before the accident. He was so handsome and polite, formal even. I liked him, but I knew it would never be a long-lasting thing. He's got a wife in Luanda.'

She turns back to look at the ceiling. 'Even after the accident, he still is terribly handsome, don't you think? Something about him. I was glad we were able to save the leg, most of it anyway. But ever since, it's been over between us. It changes things.'

Lena does not say anything. Words have been difficult since the afternoon. She wonders if DJ knew about Jeanette and Carlos. What is DJ doing now? Is she alone somewhere in the dark? Is she trying to get in touch, or to get away? Why isn't she here in Quessa, with the team, where she belongs?

The moon shines through one window and turns the ceiling rafters into clashes of angular shadows. The clinic smells of antiseptic and bad breath, from whispers, shouts and moaned problems.

'Lena?'

She does not turn towards Jeanette, hoping she will stop talking.

'How many people did we treat today?'

She pretends she needs a moment to remember. 'Ninety-seven, including Avelina's daughter.'

'Right. Ninety-seven people who you helped. With me, of course, but I couldn't have done it without you.'

She starts to cry silently. She wishes Jeanette would just leave her be.

Jeanette reaches over and pulls her into a hug. The smell of Jeanette's sweat and fading shampoo are overpowering. Her large breasts press up against Lena's lean body and there's no way to get away from the embrace.

Her cries come out in moans as she shudders into Jeanette. She can feel her saliva and tears soaking into her friend's shirt but she can't pull back and doesn't care.

Thirty-two

Kojo is up before the sun. Adrenaline propels his thoughts and by the time the others are awake he has worked up a plan with priorities, actions and timelines. They need to join up with the community organisers to get a better sense of the overall numbers of new arrivals, and where they are settling. Find out if they are planning to stay in Quessa or move on. He has to alert the UN and WFP to coordinate food rations and other supplies, hopefully shipments can accelerate this week. The team here must plan new sanitation zones and water piping to prevent the spread of disease or – God forbid – cholera. The scale is daunting, but the actions – one step at a time – he can visualise and set in an orderly timetable. It's manageable... just. With a bit of trust and good logistics backup.

Jeanette wakes and rubs her eyes. 'I need a cuppa.'

There is a knock at the door. '*Chá! Biscoitos! Alguém tem fome?*' Nuria calls out.

Kojo sees Lena stand up slowly and move towards the door. He catches her elbow. 'Lena,' he says, trying to read her face, but her look is hard to interpret. 'I didn't have the chance to say, you stepped up to do a really important job yesterday.'

She pulls her arm away and shakes her head. 'I don't know

why I was sick with the chocolate bar,' she says. 'I hope it didn't put you off.'

'It takes more than that to come down in my esteem,' he says. 'No, truly, you rose to the occasion really well. Jeanette says you were brilliant. And we didn't have the chance to give you any training in health or sanitation. So, thank you.'

'It's no problem; there's so much work to do that I want to help.' She looks at him directly, and her brown eyes are big like a child's, lids swollen with sleep and expectation.

He has to look away. 'But today,' he says, 'there's something that you are particularly well placed to do. I wondered if we could use your skills as a photographer. Would you be willing to do that?'

She smiles, and seems to wake up that much more.

He continues, 'It would be ideal if you could help people with identification. Many people have lost track of loved ones, or have given birth here with no record. That woman, Avelina, for example. Her baby needs some documentation. Also, there are many others, those who have been displaced and have missing family members. Would you be willing to set up some rudimentary system for tracing?'

She nods with energy, but then breaks away from him casually. 'Let me have a wash and I'll see what I can do,' she says.

'That would be wonderful, Lena,' he says to her as she walks away.

'Whatever, boss. You're in charge,' she says back over her shoulder.

He watches her go to the water table. He heard her sobbing last night. Jeanette smoothed things over in the end. He chides himself for ever imagining he could be the one to reach out to her and make her feel better, this enigmatic woman from London. It is so unexpected that someone like her has been dropped here in the middle of this conflict zone. But he needs to hide away the feeling that he very much wants her to stay.

In any case, there is no time for personal matters. There is a huge amount of work to do. He must look after the whole team. Today they will have a warm meal before starting and they must break for lunch; he will arrange something with the local leaders. And they will leave camp before curfew, have a rest day before coming back. You have to look after your people, he knows. If you don't have your team, you have nothing.

'*Esta é Esperança Martinho.*' Lucia introduces the one-day old baby.

Lena holds back tears as she writes the name solemnly on an improvised birth certificate. She hopes Avelina would be happy. Let's hope, wherever she is now, that she can forgive them for failing to save her.

She asks Lucia to hold up a number next to the child and then she takes the photo. In a notebook, she writes the child's name and the family's original home village, indexed. Later, she hopes to download the photos to a team laptop and print them up somehow. She has the idea of a template to give back to people some kind of an ID card – she hasn't worked out all the details yet, but it should be possible with the printer back in the villa.

News gets out that a photographer wants to help people trace their lost family members. A cluster of interested people gathers, clucking comments and general approval. They press forward with their requests. The faces relax when they see they will each have their moment with the camera.

By lunchtime there are hundreds of people keen to get their photos taken. Nuria reminds Lena to drink water and to stop to eat a quick lunch. Otherwise she has attention only for the people in front of her, one at a time or in family groups. She ensures that they are in the shade, no distorting shadows, no distracting background. No smiles if they choose. Each one an individual, with their features, their scars, their stories.

'*Ola minha amiga,*' a voice says softly, snapping Lena out of automatic mode. It's Fernanda; Lena recognises the vivid green eyes. Her daughter's eyes, too, have the same hue. Lena feels embarrassed about how she acted last time, until she reads acceptance on Fernanda's face. The mother pulls her three children into the position for a family ID shot.

Fernanda reminds her: '*Eu e tu somos iguais.*' We are the same, you and I. Both searching for a sister. Lena remembers the story about Kudielela and promises that she will make extra prints. She will find a way to bring them back to the camp as soon as possible.

That afternoon, back on the road, Lena and the others fall silent. They are dirty, worked to exhaustion, but each of them holds their own satisfaction from the past two days. There was no room for alternative choices. No time for indecision. Just actions taken against a landscape of dramatic need.

Thirty-three

'What I don't get,' Brad says, back at the villa that evening, 'is why we have so many people from all the countryside around these northern provinces, but none from Luremo Sul.'

The others don't look up from their pasta.

'Lena, you've been taking down names and locations. Have you had any from Luremo Sul?'

'Can't say it's come up a lot.'

'Maybe the next time someone says they're from near there, ask some questions.'

'Hey Brad, wait a minute,' Kojo says. 'That is not Lena's job.'

'I know, but what y'all keep forgetting is that we don't have a communications officer, so nobody's triangulating this information.' Brad steps away from the table and unfolds a large map onto the floor. 'Come on, take a look.'

Not willing to let go of her dinner, Lena stands with her pasta bowl and looks at the roads and boundaries of the highlands she's starting to be familiar with.

'See? Saurimo, Lucapa, Andulo – these are all names we've been hearing these past few days, am I right?' He looks around for confirmation.

'There was that last push from UNITA on the road between

Munhango and Luena,' Jeanette says. 'I had some bullet-wounds to be treated from that. Old, infected ones, I'm afraid. Sorry if that puts you off your food.'

'And Cuango was empty when we visited the day before yesterday,' Kojo adds.

Lena puts down the pasta and gets on her hands and knees. She has always loved maps, since she was young. They are like blueprints for landscape photography, with so many possibilities for future compositions. She examines the geometric beauty of the lines showing boundaries, elevation, settlements and dried river beds. 'Why are you interested in Luremo Sul?' she asks.

'There's a famous diamond catchment there,' Kojo says. 'One rumoured to never run out.'

'Very close to the border with Congo,' she observes.

'Close enough for anybody to walk,' Brad says.

'Soldiers?' she asks.

'Young ones,' Brad says.

'Or civilians,' Jeanette adds. 'Threatened.'

'Threatened with…?' Lena presses.

'People are forced to make an impossible choice: give up your son or the girls all get raped, that kind of thing. The girls often get raped anyway, just to show who has the power.'

'And no one says anything?'

'Would you? They are traumatised, ashamed and hurting,' Jeanette says. 'Would you find it easy to talk to a stranger about that, in your second or third language?'

Lena shakes her head.

Jeanette continues, 'It's easier to say "I can't see out of my right eye", or "my daughter is so weak", than to say what happened to you on the road from Munhango.'

'But the war is over,' Lena says. 'What can UNITA do for much longer? Their supplies must run out soon.'

'Maybe,' Brad says, 'no one has told them that yet.'

'There was something I wanted to tell you guys,' Jeanette says. Her words slur a bit with tiredness, but she still keeps talking. 'The rumours, about the nurses hurting people, remember that? What Jake was telling us?'

Lena hates hearing his name.

'I heard it again, this time from people who looked really frightened. Of me! Can you imagine. "*Sem picadas, por favor!*" she said, this woman, a mother of three and another one on the way. No stinging… What in heaven's name do you think they were talking about?'

'Stinging, like needles?' Lena asks.

'Or like a snake. Another patient – a boy this time, on his own, lost all his family – pulled his arm away from me and said, "*Sem veneno de cobra.*" Why would he be worried about snake venom?'

'Maybe UNITA has been circulating the rumours, trying to get people afraid to seek outside help?' Brad says.

'We've had tension with UNITA before, but never with people afraid to get treatment.'

'Were they new patients, or ones you had seen before?' Kojo asks.

'I think they had been before. The mum had a vaccination card for the kids. But I didn't see them, Maria did.'

Lena leans closer to make sure she is hearing it clearly. 'Maria did? When?'

'Her last clinics, in Quessa, or maybe Luremo.'

'Isn't that the one you were having trouble with the figures on, Brad?' Lena asks.

'How the heck do you know about that?'

'You were muttering about it, when I first arrived. You were too distracted to say hello properly.'

'Yeah, that clinic had much lower figures of attendance. Actually, nearly zero. I think Maria forgot to save the data. Deleted it by accident or something.'

'Or something…' She stands up and walks back and forth behind the couch for a moment. 'Is there anything else Maria could have been doing, that people might have been afraid of?'

'You never had the chance to meet her,' Kojo says, 'or else you would not ask that kind of question.'

'But you said – didn't you, Jeanette – that she was concerned about maternal-to-infant HIV transmission, right? Said she was hoping to trial a new test or something like that?'

Jeanette nods.

'Does the test involve needles?'

'Most of them do.'

'Was it possible she was trying to start this, and UNITA decided to whip up some rumours, taking their opportunity to scare people away from contact with humanitarians?'

'I like your thinking, Lena,' Brad says. 'You're starting to get into the twisted logic of this place.'

'That could explain why no one showed up for clinic, possibly. Or why someone might have a grudge against a nurse, if someone died in childbirth or something. However wrong it is, people could believe it.'

'Maybe,' Jeanette says, 'the rebels needed a rationale to convince a large number of people to move to another place in a hurry. But I dunno. People say the strangest things at different times in this war. Panic gets them fidgety and strange. I'm sure if Maria was trying to do the blood samples, she would've explained it to the mothers, about preventing the transmission to the babies, keeping them well. But I don't think she would have started much of that. She didn't really have time before…' She doesn't finish the sentence, gets up and leaves the room.

They can't yet retreat into sleep. Candles are lit, placed on dishes. Lena slumps into the couch. A few weeks earlier she had not seen the inside of this villa. Now it feels like her place.

Jeanette's face across the room is tinted by the golden-pink of the candle, nearly matching her bright hair colour. She twirls a lock around her finger again and again, as if flirting with an old memory. The other hand is light on Brad's shoulder. He sits on the floor at her feet, staring into the candle and nursing a beer.

Kojo sits on the couch next to Lena. The way the candles dance about, he is mostly in shadow. His hand rests on the leather, just a few centimetres away from hers.

'What's this music?' Lena asks.

'Brazilian, I think,' Jeanette says.

'No – from Cape Verde,' says Brad.

'I like it,' Lena says. The singer's voice is low and soothing, with a strong beat that makes it more urgent. She gets up to get another drink. In the fridge there is beer, Coke, bottles of filtered water and vaccines for the children wedged across the top shelf. 'Anyone want another beer?' she calls out. 'There's three left.'

'How about something a bit stronger?' asks Brad. He points to a bottle of rum. 'And the Cokes?' She brings them back to the coffee table. Jeanette takes the bottles from her and pours four short shots of the rum, before splashing some Coke into the glasses and a bit on the table.

Lena sits back on the sofa and rolls the glass around between her palms. The smell of the rum – so sugary, a bit sickening. Brings to mind adolescence, Lucien, messy nights and misunderstandings. Best not to go there.

*

'Maria's family is from near Luremo, remember?' Kojo says. 'That's why we assigned her to the clinic there. We thought people would trust her, open up to her.' He pauses for a sip. 'I asked her to keep her ear to the ground, let us know if she heard anything about troops moving or new displacement. But I didn't realise that it might have put her in a tricky position.'

'What do you mean?' Lena asks.

'I don't know. Maybe we asked too much. The last time she was there, with DJ leading the engineers, something wasn't right.'

There's no reply, as the CD finishes the song. There is a pause before it flips back to the beginning and starts again.

'Could I ask…' Lena starts.

The rum makes a smooth warmth in Kojo's throat. 'Hmm?'

'Were they always a couple, from the beginning?'

He sighs. He doesn't like going back to that time in his mind. 'Not always,' he says. He runs his tongue over his teeth. He feels like he could share, a bit. 'There was a kind of transition period, I would say.'

'Once she met DJ,' Jeanette interrupts, 'it was pretty much set.'

'Maria just had this way with people,' Brad comes in. 'But for most people it was like welcoming you into her family. As a cousin, or something.'

'But when those two met, something was different,' Kojo says. 'Everyone else was forgotten.'

'DJ rotated into Malanje,' Brad says, 'and right away they were inseparable. Maria didn't change, exactly, but you had to admit when you saw her it was as if she had been waiting for DJ her whole life.'

'She was so beautiful and approachable,' Jeanette says. 'She could have had any of the men around. But no one ever got close for very long. Until DJ.'

'They moved in together very quickly,' Kojo says. 'And then I heard Maria talking about DJ as her husband. She even said that to me once, when DJ and I were heading out to Quessa together: "Kojo, please take care of *meu marido*."'

He remembers the way she looked at him when she said it. As if she expected him to understand the weight of the words, the value she placed on them. And that she would never place that kind of value on him. Never did, never would.

He wishes he had never fallen for her. Life would have been so much less complicated if he had just resisted. Held back. Or just simply not let himself believe the illusion that she might have been the one for him.

'They worked together all the time, on their own, without back up,' Jeanette says. 'Maybe something happened in Luremo that they couldn't tell anyone, and were trying to deal with alone.'

'I should have rotated them somewhere else in the country, for a time,' Kojo says, bringing his mind back to thinking about protocols. That was a more neutral line of thought. 'Away from people who knew her, who maybe wanted something from her. For their own protection.'

'Don't blame yourself, Kojo,' Jeanette says. She has said the words dozens of times since the accident, but it does no good.

'I should have seen this coming,' he says.

'Seen what coming?' Lena asks.

The room goes quiet as each of them ponder the different possible answers to the question. The candles flicker, refusing to favour one person over another.

Thirty-four

You start to make a plan.

You can't tell anyone.

Even with the nuns, there's no one you can really trust. They've looked after your body, hoping to also save your soul. But you know you are ruined beyond repair. If God cared about you, he would have found a way to save Maria, or to have killed you both at the same time.

You don't have time for God any more. You are running out of time.

You feel stronger, now that the malaria has passed. But you know you have shed weight, lost muscle. There's not much of you now. You wonder if you are strong enough to steer the bike.

Steer it where? That's the question.

How much petrol is in the tank? You wish you had checked. Now if anyone saw you near the machine, they would be suspicious.

They are kind, these women. You know why Maria loved them.

Congolese music comes in through the thin walls of your room. You know it from your time in Maria's home village on the border. It makes your heart ache, yet your sad limbs want to get up and dance at the same time.

You wonder how long you have before someone comes looking for you. Your instinct is to keep running. But before you go, no unusual behaviour, nothing to raise a question. Then make your escape, before anyone can stop you.

Thirty-five

'Charlie Whisky One, Charlie Whisky One, this is Charlie Whisky Twelve,' Kojo says into the radio. 'Do you copy?"

Some urgent messages have come in for Lena from the British Embassy. Confidential. He goes to get her.

'Is it about DJ?' she asks, as she bounds up the stairs two at a time to avoid the gaps she hardly even notices any more.

He fits her up with the headphones and microphone, then steps back. He knows he should leave the room and give her privacy, but he can't quite bring himself to do it. His back rests on the door frame, to look as if he is intending to go. He tries to read her face while he hears her side of the conversation.

'This is Charlie Whisky Nineteen,' she says. 'Can you hear me?'

He watches her expression as she listens. She squints and looks into the equipment, as if trying to read something tiny.

Who is it? Is it from home? Will she have to leave? Lord, please don't make her leave, not just yet.

She is nodding, and eventually her serious expression folds into a smile. She looks up at him and he has to smile too.

'Yes, I copy,' she is saying. 'Thank you for that. And the other one?'

She holds her hands over the headphones, as if trying to filter out interference. She continues to nod, then bursts out laughing.

'Well, many thanks for that one too,' she says. 'I'll think about what to send back to him in the next couple of days... Is that all?' she asks the operator. Then she gestures to Kojo to ask if he wants to get back on. He shakes his head.

'Okay, over and out,' she says, and takes off the headphones. 'A bit difficult to hear, but I think I got the hang of it.'

He tries to sound casual. 'So, what was so urgent?'

'One was from the embassy staff dealing with Jake's case. He's been released and deported. They confirmed that there was no further mistreatment, although he was still proclaiming total innocence.'

'He may be telling the truth.'

'Maybe, but I think he was never as discreet as he thought he was. He's not journalist material. He stood out everywhere he went, but thought he was subtle. Comes from being arrogant through and through.'

'Aren't you being a bit harsh on a man who has just spent more than a week in an Angolan prison?'

'Perhaps... but I can't shake the idea that he may have endangered DJ and Maria. I don't like the man, not at all.'

'DJ did not like him either. You have more in common than you thought.'

She rewards him with a big smile, bigger than he has seen in days.

'And there was a second message?'

'Yes, from Lucien.'

'He tracked you down – what was so funny?'

'Oh, nothing really. He misses me. I've never been away so long. Says I abandoned him with the wankers and the drunks.'

'Worried for you?'

'Hmmm...' She looks past him and starts to move around him.

'Lena, wait,' he says. 'I heard that UNITA forces have vacated the roads between Cuango and Luremo Sul. We can go on to try to track down Maria's family if you want.'

'What about Quessa?'

'Brad can lead tomorrow in Quessa. You were right – we need to keep moving and find DJ, before it gets more unpredictable.'

Her face is more animated than he has seen in such a long time. He would do anything for that look.

'So, to Luremo we go.' He puts his hands on both her shoulders to look at her straight on. 'Are you sure you want to? It is hard to know the security situation.'

'We'll go. Of course we'll go.'

Lena packs a small backpack. Just one camera and canisters of film, leaving the digital one behind. One notebook, pens, water bottle and iodine, one change of clothes. But she has nothing sentimental from London for DJ. She should have brought something from Mum or Dad. Or a childhood photo of them as a family.

Out in the dining area, no one is around. She quickly brings down the group photograph where DJ has her arm around Maria. In it, the whole CWA team is there, people she knows now: Nuria, Jeanette, Andreas. Kojo is near Maria with his face tilted in her direction, but he is the one person not smiling at whatever grand laugh the others are sharing. She slips the photo out of the frame, and tucks it into the last pages of her notebook.

*

She's not able to sleep. She goes over the words from the radio dispatcher. Jake, now on his way to London. He always maintained his complete conviction about conspiracies swirling around Malanje, thought he would make his mark breaking the story. The time with him now feels like a distant encounter with an awkward relation, one she wants to forget. But what if he was right about people here? Carlos, Kojo, the pilot...? Who can you trust, if they all are connected somehow?

She closes her eyes. Her hands come up to her face. She massages circles, tracing the line from her eyebrows to the crescent below her eye sockets. Her eyes have been working hard to focus for the past two days. She wishes they would just go blurry for a moment and then into sweet darkness.

She remembers Lucien kissing her there, at the concave bit to the side of her forehead. The temple – the entrance to the face, from the side. She would let him, sometimes, get close. Lie with her on the sofa bed, already made up for sleep.

'Everything packed now?' he'd asked. She played with the tattoo he'd chosen on his eighteenth birthday, weaving up the inside of his forearm. Did he ever regret the choices made back then? They'd never discussed it.

'Passport, check. Malaria meds, check,' she said. 'But no clue what I'm going to do when I get there.'

'You'll be all right. Always have been.'

'But what if everything falls apart?'

'You're a clever one, you'll think of something.'

She stopped tracing the blue–black lines for a moment, moved a few inches away. He brought his skin closer again, wanted it to keep going. She resumed the swirling, the sensation like a meditation.

'And if you get in trouble, you find a way to call old boy

Lucien.' He came up on his elbow to look at her. 'You can depend on me, Lena. You know that, right?'

She nodded, not looking directly at him. She knew he wanted her to, but she couldn't.

He concentrated too much on her. Knew too much. He'd been with her through everything so far, thought that her story was already half-written and he had an idea of what the rest would be. But she didn't feel the same way.

As sleep started to come, she felt him put an arm loosely around her waist, pretending to do it in a dream. She grunted, hoping he wouldn't push it. After a moment he pulled her tighter, murmuring. She heard the sheets rustle as he rolled onto his side, facing her. She refused to open her eyes.

He kissed her again, on the ear, and below it. He moved to give her kisses down her neck, and then to that dip above the clavicle. He knew she liked that. His hips pressed against her and she recognised the motions he used to do, seeing if she'd reciprocate.

She moved away. 'No, Lucien…'

He exhaled and pulled his arm away. Then shifted his legs off the side of the couch. His back to her, she could see his thin frame curved over, chin in his hands. He was shaking his head back and forth slowly.

'Sorry, it's just—'

'You're a ball-breaker, you know that?' he said. He got up and fished around in the dark, finding a pack of cigarettes on the coffee table. A lighter clicked. It lit up his face in streaks that made him look older and leaner than before. 'Always have been.'

'Forgive me, hon. Just can't tonight.'

'You'll come running back to me, you know that.' He looked out at the room, not at her. 'Always do.'

She wasn't so sure, not this time.

Part IV

Part IV

Thirty-six

The road has a familiar feel. The heat, the dust, even the constant game of surveying the ground for changes feels normal now to Lena. Pursuing DJ is what she is meant to do.

Kojo stops the bike for a moment. 'The road forks ahead,' he says. 'One way leads to Luremo Sul, the other to a nunnery.'

'Nuns, out here?'

'Why, you think people here don't need God any more?'

'Not that. I just thought the conditions would be quite... rough.'

'Nothing would stop those women,' he says. 'They fight everything with love. If we don't find DJ in Luremo Sul, it is another place she might be.'

'DJ? I can't imagine her at a nunnery. She had so many issues with the church growing up.'

'People can change, with different circumstances.'

'Not that much, surely.'

They pass other abandoned villages, no sign of people. The lack of dirt on the windows and the scratches across the corrugated iron make it seem like the people are not long gone.

'Where is everybody?' she shouts, but she's not sure if he hears.

They are surprised by a bus ahead at the next curve. He doesn't have time to change course, but he pulls the bike to the very edge of the road and leans away. The horn blasts as the bus roars past, the tyres breaking up the dried ridges of mud. They are showered with soil.

'Are you all right?' he asks, rubbing his helmet clean with his sleeve.

She looks at the back of the bus. From the rear window peer a dozen young faces, as puzzled about her as she is to see them.

'Where are they going?' she asks.

'Where are they coming from? That's what I want to know.'

'And only children on board?'

He doesn't answer. He has a sharp sense of foreboding about this section of road. He never should have offered to bring her here. Before he re-starts the engine, he tries to think of any reason why they must turn back, something strong enough to convince her. He should be protecting her, not bringing her deeper into the conflict. But he can't seem to change tack.

'Let's take a break,' he suggests, coming off the bike and putting down the kickstand.

They take off their helmets and share a drink. He catches himself watching her lips on the edge of the bottle, and turns away.

He tells her the first thing he can think of. 'When I was a boy, I was always climbing trees. Our village was at a crossroads. It was Ashanti land, between the trading routes north to the Sahara, and the road to Accra and the sea. Between the sand and the sea, that's how we felt.

'It was dry and hot, a lot like this. I think that's why I always felt at home in Malanje, from the start. And the lorries came through, big ones for the timber trade. They came in these convoys of three or four that would rustle up so much dust. So when I heard them coming, I would scramble up my favourite tree and climb high. That way I could look out and see what was coming, and be above the winds and dust.'

She has an amused expression on her face. 'Do you still want to climb trees to get away from it all?'

'Too heavy now,' he laughs and hits a hand against his stomach. 'I would weigh them all down, more than the fattest mango you ever saw.'

She laughs too. 'That would have to be a really fat mango.'

He likes bringing her into his stories. Then his hopes fall. He wishes they were together somewhere else, anywhere else.

She nods to him that she has had enough water, and swings her leg back over the motorcycle. It is clear she expects them to go on.

He sees it too late, as they come around a curve. He sits up straight and jerks the bike to a halt.

'What is it?' she asks.

'Why would there still be checkpoints?' he says, too quietly for her to hear. 'Has no one told them the war is over?'

Ahead of them are a number of boys holding machine guns, all pointed at the motorcycle. They seem to be protecting a shack by the side of the road, and a rope chain is drawn up.

They are less than twenty metres from the boys. There is no way to hide or turn back. His mind races to try to find any other option, but there is none. He stops the bike, puts his feet down to the road and holds his hands up.

The boys are startled and fidget with the guns, shouting for their leader and arguing.

The door of the shack opens with a creak. A man with a wide hat and a cane emerges. He looks at them on the motorcycle and is motionless for a moment. He says, louder, '*Ah merda.*'

Some of the boys giggle, but stop with a stern look from the man.

'Carlos,' Kojo says to himself.

'Kojo, my friend, what in the devil's name are you doing out here?'

He is about to explain, but prefers to keep quiet while the guns are trained on him. Child soldiers can be touchy with the trigger.

After a moment, when the boys still haven't relaxed, he says loudly, 'Could you please tell them to put the guns aside? For a humanitarian mission.'

Carlos says something quietly to the boys. They reluctantly lower their guns, but keep glaring at Kojo and Lena.

'Shall we approach?' Kojo asks.

'No need to be so formal, my friend. Please, come take a coffee.' Carlos turns his back on them and walks into the shack, expecting to be followed.

Kojo looks at Lena. His heart is beating so loudly in his ears he has trouble hearing her as she whispers something to him. He covers it up with a 'Yes, yes… we do not have any choice.'

Inside the shack are two chairs, a table and a small sink. A makeshift hob holds a tiny tea kettle. Carlos moves a few papers and a crumpled shirt from the centre of the table to its edge to make space for them to have coffee. The room is otherwise bare except for a stack of crates. It smells of old cigarettes and rotting fruit.

Carlos leans on his good leg and rests his cane at his hip. He lights a match to boil the kettle. Satisfied with the flame, he swings around and sits in the closest chair. The cane clatters to the ground. He offers the second chair to them. Kojo takes a seat; Lena stands.

She thinks back to the government flag under the stale air conditioning when they first met. But this shack is not the police headquarters; there are no MPLA symbols. No sign of state control, agreed by politicians far away.

What did Jake say the last time she saw him? Carlos is notorious for playing all sides of the game, he'd said, his face showing no sarcasm.

'My friend, I wasn't expecting to see you here, so far from town,' Carlos says.

Kojo remains silent. When the kettle whistles Carlos stands up again, without the cane this time, and walks with difficulty to the hob.

'Just boiled,' he explains, pouring the water and quickly mixing in some instant coffee. The mug doesn't look like it's been cleaned, but Kojo accepts it. She shakes her head.

'With all the work in Quessa,' Carlos says, 'I thought you'd be based there for some time.'

'We were in Quessa,' Lena says.

Carlos looks at her, surprised.

She adds, 'I mean, Kojo led the team back there. I was helping out as a photographer.'

'Photographer? Is that what you are here for?' Carlos frowns. It makes him look ugly. His face was sculpted for something different, used to getting his own way. 'I thought you were in Luanda, with that Lansdowne fellow.'

'We are here looking for DJ, remember my engineer?' Kojo says.

'Or news about the man who fled the accident, who you mentioned,' she says.

Kojo winces. She looks at him, puzzled, then back to Carlos.

He blinks a few times, looking at both of them, as if he's owed some explanation.

'Don't you have any leads?' she asks.

Carlos blows over his coffee before he speaks. 'Kojo, I thought you would have shared the information,' Carlos says.

'What information?' She looks from Carlos to Kojo.

Carlos takes a moment to light a new cigarette. Smoke lingers in the air in an S-shape before it dissipates. 'My dear, what Kojo isn't telling you, is that it's perfectly clear that there was no man fleeing the scene of the accident. We cleared that up days ago.'

She takes a step backwards, then steadies herself by leaning on the table. 'What do you mean?'

'My men at the time saw a man flee, but this was no stranger. When we met before, I hadn't had a chance to interview them properly. Now, as I explained to Kojo, the description perfectly matches DJ.'

'DJ, you mean my DJ?' she says.

'The one and only,' Carlos says.

'Is that true?' she asks Kojo. 'You already knew?'

'Of course he did,' Carlos says. 'I told him three days ago on the radio. He is responsible for CWA staff in this country. But he asked for more time to try to reach DJ, I suspect to see if he would turn himself in. Is that what you're attempting to do now?'

'No, no, no.' She staggers and then steadies herself with legs in a more stable stance. 'You can't mean DJ.'

'I was waiting for the right moment to tell you,' Kojo says.

She feels the blood rise to her face, pulsing at her temples as she shakes her head. 'It's not true. Can't be.'

'Probably a lover's spat,' Carlos says.

'I'm not sure if that's the truth,' Kojo says. 'We'll only know when we find DJ.'

'I have plenty of witnesses who can testify to DJ's temper,' Carlos says. 'Particularly after drinking.'

'But DJ didn't do it!' She tries not to shout but can't help herself. 'A temper, yes. But never violent! Not towards people, not towards someone... Surely if you know DJ you know that!'

'You are a good judge of character, Kojo,' Carlos says. 'You must have sensed it. DJ was always a bit odd.'

She leans heavily on the table and feels it wobble beneath her. 'DJ wasn't odd,' she says quietly. 'Just made different choices from other people.'

Carlos refuses to argue. He exhales, turning it into a sigh. She hates him in that moment.

'And what do we do now, my friends?' he says.

'We're going to find DJ,' she says. 'Then you'll have your explanation for what happened, and you'll know DJ is innocent.'

'But he's not here, is he?' Carlos waves his arms around the small shack.

'We would like to go on our way to Luremo Sul, if you don't mind,' Kojo says. 'Maria had family there. Lena would like to talk with them.' He gets up out of the chair.

'Ah yes, well you see, I do mind. Luremo Sul is under close surveillance, for criminal activities. It's not safe for people like you.'

'Carlos,' Kojo rumbles.

'I could let you continue, but with police protection.'

'You know we do not usually travel with armed escort, Carlos.'

'Well, these are unusual times, are they not? Lots of dangerous bandits around, and you wouldn't want to risk young Lena's security, would you?'

Kojo shakes his head.

'Decided then. We'll go together. I'd like to see DJ as well. But I don't think you'll find what you're looking for in Luremo.'

'We'll see,' Lena says. She feels so angry at the deception and obstructions that she could scream, but swallows hard instead to keep it down. As she straightens up, the table lurches and items fall to the ground. It is not just clothing and papers; there is the sound of something metallic hitting the floor.

When she reaches down to pick up the things she's knocked off, Carlos says, 'No, leave that!'

'It's no big deal,' she says, picking up the papers and some cloth. Out falls something made up of a brass chain and a loop, with two small brass containers hanging from it. She lifts it and sees that it is a miniature set of scales. She can't think what it would be needed for, this far away from the market.

'That's no concern of yours,' Carlos says, looking at her as if she is a naughty child. He snatches it out of her hand and puts it back on the table. Kojo's face is grey and unreadable as she turns to leave the shack.

Thirty-seven

Carlos agrees that Kojo and Lena can ride behind the armed vehicle. Kojo steers the bike carefully, giving some space between the car and them.

He has made a serious mistake bringing her into this situation. He should have come alone. Or with Sebastião, who can negotiate his way out of anything. He didn't know that Carlos was involved with the diamond racket. Diamonds are UNITA's business, everyone knows that. And now the highest MPLA authority in this area is at the top of that pyramid?

Carlos is the Big Man out here, with the scales for smuggling and the child soldiers protecting him. Kojo is dismayed that it has come to this. He's always known that Carlos had his own agenda, and was probably earning a little something on top of the meagre salary he sends home to his wife in Luanda. Now he realises how wrong his instincts have been. He had been sure that Carlos held in him some sense of service, as a policeman and having served in the army. Some sense of fighting a just war against the rebels, for the right reasons. But finding him in the cabin with the diamond equipment has proved all that to be a veneer, with the truth badly hidden.

He is alarmed that he got it so wrong. How could he not

have sensed it? They have been close, arguably very close. He's trusted him. Earned his trust in return. Thought they were men not too different from each other.

What else has he misjudged? Who else has been hurt, on his watch?

Carlos is clever. He wouldn't be sloppy. He would have the whole place organised to suit himself. But he was not expecting witnesses. Surely he is working on a plan as he drives. Kojo just needs to be one step ahead of it.

Lena clutches tightly onto Kojo's waist as they head towards Luremo Sul, with no choice but to follow Carlos's car. She wants to squeeze Kojo tighter, to hurt him a bit even as she has to depend on him. How could he hold out on her another time? Does that mean he suspects DJ too? How could he? Does he know nothing about her? Or maybe he is wrapped up in this diamonds scheme as well. She can't imagine Kojo getting involved in such a thing, but she has to admit she doesn't really know him at all.

She recognises that a few intense days together have brought a certain intimacy, but that could all be an act. You think you know someone, you start to have feelings for them, and then something else is revealed, or even just hinted at. People can have all sorts of things they hide from each other.

The landscape changes as they turn towards a river valley. The dusty red-brown of the parched road becomes veiled in greenery, with ferns reaching out into their path and vines lacing overhead. It sounds different, as the motorcycle noises become absorbed by the foliage. Everything feels muffled, anything but safe.

'Is this where DJ was heading?' she shouts into his ear.

He shakes his head in the helmet, looking forward.

'What's the plan?' she shouts louder.

'Stay alert. Be ready to get out quick if we need.'

The vehicles come into an abandoned town. Empty vendors' shacks line the road, no longer trying to sell to customers who are not coming. Windows of houses near the road are black and she sees no life inside.

Carlos's car pulls into the gates of a school, and Kojo brings the motorcycle inside the fence and onto the grass. The driver of the car leaves the engine running as Carlos and two armed boys get out. The guns are aimed at Kojo and Lena.

'You will wait here,' Carlos says.

'Where is everybody?' she asks. Carlos ignores her.

'We just want to talk to the Pereira family,' Kojo says. 'Maria's sister?'

Carlos gives Kojo an annoyed look as he gets back in the car.

'Please, Carlos,' Kojo says. 'It is very important.'

'You shouldn't have come, Kojo.' Carlos shuts the door, and the driver puts the engine into reverse. One of the armed boys shuts and bolts the gate behind, locking Lena and Kojo in the compound.

Kojo turns to her. 'My God...' he says, arms falling to his sides.

The school is made up of slabs of grey concrete just one storey high, with iron poles pointing out of the corners reaching up to another level not yet built. Corrugated iron sheets balance on top, held down by occasional bricks or stones. A staircase starts on the ground and arrives at the top for no purpose. The classrooms have no glass in the windows.

The guards turn their backs to Kojo and Lena. They start to smoke, relaxed now that their boss has left. Kojo leads Lena away from the gate and they enter an empty classroom. There are no benches or tables, just a bare concrete floor. He slumps into a corner with his back against the rough wall.

'Lena…' he starts, but does not continue.

'You could have told me,' she says.

'I was going to.'

'How can I believe you? Outrageous that you'd hold that back. Can't fucking believe it.'

'You have got to know—'

'Know what? That you men hold your cards close to your chest? Until you lose track of them, then what?'

'It was—'

'What else are you and Carlos keeping to yourselves?' She is shouting and hates the sound of her voice bouncing off the concrete walls, but she can't stop. 'This is my sister we're talking about! To you it's just a job, maybe, but – this is her life!'

'And yours?'

She pauses. No, not her life. Not her story. It was never her story.

More quietly, she says, 'She didn't do it, you know that.'

'Of course not. He just said that because he feels guilty about not investigating Maria's death properly. He's on the defensive.'

'Anything else you're holding out on me?'

'No, God no – Lena…' His face tilts down to his hands. He looks unsettled and powerless. 'I had no idea we would end up here.'

'What did you expect?'

'I didn't expect anything, not Carlos, not this…'

'He didn't tell you?' She looks closely at him. She still has faith that you can read a man's face and know if he is telling a lie. Something would twitch or twist. But his face is calm, sad, dismayed. Disillusioned. It reminds her of her father for some reason, but she doesn't know why. He is not lying, she is sure of it.

Quieter now, she says, 'So you don't know what he's planning?'

He shakes his head.

She looks out of the window at the boys standing guard. 'DJ wouldn't do anything like that,' she says. 'She is a protector type. Always has been. Fiercely so. You should know that.'

He recedes into his mind, in the same way she saw at Quessa camp a few days earlier. Before he had a plan.

'Do you think Carlos knows where she is?'

No response.

She puts her elbows on the window ledge. She senses moisture and tension in the air. Storm coming. You can trust in that.

Thirty-eight

It comes down heavy and determined. From her position in the abandoned classroom, she can see that the armed boys have left their post to find shelter. The rain punches the ground, making ripples in the puddles and craters in the mud. It is powerful, particularly as the ground was so desiccated. Before long, the water forms a shallow river over the paths and begins to pool at the door of the classroom.

Night falls. She and Kojo have spoken very little.

Suddenly, beams of headlamps shine through the rain, coming through gaps in the fence. The driver sounds the horn and she sees one of the guards run forward to unlock the gate, shielding his head from the rain with a plastic bag.

Into the school yard comes an antiquated bus that slumps into the mud then stops. The door squeals open and out come dozens of children of different heights and sizes. In filthy clothes weighed down by the rain, they sag with weariness. An older child helps a smaller one come down the steps of the bus, but then appears to run out of strength. The younger child tries to hold the other's hand, but it swings limp at his side. Instead, the smaller one holds onto the back of the shredded cloth that was once a t-shirt. They don't look left or right as they walk towards the back of the school yard.

'Kojo, listen,' she says. 'It's clear we're not going to be allowed to leave. Carlos has established his own dominion here or something. But he likes you, and respects you. And his people need to offer us some food, don't you think?'

He nods.

'Why don't you go and ask? Can't hurt.'

'I need to think of a strategy,' he says.

'If we both stay here, we'll make no progress.'

He blinks slowly.

'I'll go,' she says. 'I'll see if the children will talk to me.' Before he can stop her, she closes her jacket and moves out of the classroom.

Thunder grumbles in the distance. Will there be lightning? Will a rain-soaked concrete block be safe, with those metal poles sticking up?

She follows the flow of the rainwater as it makes its way down to another level of ground. There are more concrete structures, two storeys high. Again, these buildings are unfinished, no glass or doors, with haphazard corrugated roof sheets here and there. Sheets hang in the window gaps, useless in the fight against the driving rain. Rubber boots and flip-flops are scattered near the threshold of what appears to be a communal room.

As she comes closer to the doorway, she sees Carlos's guard-boys, leaning on their guns like props. They are smoking rolled joints and look bored.

Two lanterns hang from the wall, the light falling on children sitting on the floor. So many of them, too many to count. Some are cross-legged, others curl knees towards chins. Their bodies cover the surface of the ground. She searches for the pair she saw descend the bus stairs, but can't make them out.

The children all focus on their bowls. They use cupped hands to shovel food into their mouths. Even when the bowls are empty, they keep repeating the movements, as if unable to believe it's all gone. The sparse light accentuates the sharp angles of elbows, shoulders and ankles of this small army of malnourished children.

Lena steps back into the shadows. Did anyone see her? You can't ask for food in front of children in that kind of state.

Jesus Christ, what are they going to do?

A small boy stands in the concrete doorway. At first, she can only see a silhouette: the strange geometric shape of an adult's t-shirt hanging off the shoulder of an underfed child. He steps away from the torchlight and Lena's eyes adjust. In the grey-black hues of the stormy night she can see his t-shirt shredded into strips that barely thread together. His face has round cheeks, contradicting the legs which are tight, thin muscle wound around bone, nothing to spare. It is the sweet face that makes her step out of the shadows.

He freezes like an animal with no shelter. She keeps her hands soft, turning the palms outward to show she means no harm. She sees him blink a few times, thinking. When she's sure the guards are not looking, she beckons him to her. He obeys with a few steps, no smile.

She uses the gentle Portuguese of her mother's tongue, introducing herself and asking him his name. He voices nothing but his lips twist left and right as if he is considering it. Does he understand her? Maybe not.

She touches a hand to her chest and says, 'Lena,' then points at him.

He smiles with half his mouth. 'Benedito,' he says, mimicking her motions. Blessed one, it means.

She tries again some lines in Portuguese – where is his mother? Does he have a father? – but she does not get through. He seems to be waiting for a break in the code.

How old is he? She holds up six fingers. He shakes his head. Seven fingers? No again. More? Does he think they're talking about age, or siblings or years in service? Who knows? But it's fun, a game with no words. She flashes her hands to count to twenty-four for herself and he laughs out loud.

Can anyone hear them? Probably not, with the rain on the corrugated roof. But still, she wouldn't want to get this sweet kid in trouble. Or any more trouble, she should say.

He looks at her neck. Her hand follows his gaze and touches on her St Christopher's necklace. From her mother so many years ago, for protection. The story about a man who carried a child on his back across a river, and later discovered it was Christ himself. He is the saint to protect those who are far from home, far from family. Lone children, like tentative Benedito here.

She wants to give it to him, but has a pang of worry. Can she part with it? What about when she needs protection herself? Gloria actively believed in its power; Lena is not so sure.

Does DJ have one too? She can't remember, wishes she could. Did Mum give her one, before she set out into the world? If she did, it didn't do much good. Or maybe it is protecting her sister, somehow, wherever she is.

Is there power in the necklace, or is the power in the believing?

She holds it out to him and his eyes light up. Does he want it? She unclasps it from behind her neck. She makes the circle complete again and places it over his irregularly shorn head, seeing the patches and dark spots. Bruises? Old injuries? Or parasites? She hopes this kid will be okay.

He smiles widely and she sees gaps in the teeth – could be a normal seven- or eight-year-old, in a different place, at any other time. Or maybe, to him, this place is normal. In any case, he seems keen she doesn't change her mind. He starts to turn and coil, like he will spring off if she tries to take it back. She stifles an urge to hug the child or claim anything from him.

Her hand goes as usual to the place on her neck where the necklace used to hang, and grasps nothing. It feels odd and her fingers fiddle for a moment. Then she drops it to her side and gives a shrug of her shoulders.

'It's yours now,' she says. '*Para sua proteção.*'

She can't tell if he understands a word in either language. She steps back, giving him an excuse to detach himself from the situation and go back to the other children.

'*Obrigado!*' he says with a sudden turn and runs back into the common room.

Kojo is relieved when she comes back. He has set up a torch from his knapsack, shining a perfect circle of light onto the ceiling.

She settles down next to him, sitting on top of his open jacket as protection against the cold concrete. He starts to talk and confirms what she's already sensed, that the scales they saw in the shack link Carlos to UNITA's diamond trade, even though he is the head of the MPLA police in the north. She tells him about the boys she saw, and about Benedito. Their shoulders touch and she doesn't move away.

'This is bad, isn't it?' she asks.

He isn't ready to answer.

'Hold me?'

He reaches out and puts one arm around her. She leans in closer and holds his hand in hers. She rubs slow circles around his big knuckle as he starts to talk.

'It's my fault,' he says. He feels her ribcage move as she breathes. It is a light structure, doesn't feel sturdy enough. 'I should have saved Maria, you see. Should have found a way to get that Medevac. All those contacts, all those people I have entertained and assisted and flattered – not one of them would come through for a dying woman.' He looks at the circle of light on the ceiling, wavering with a low battery. 'I do not know if DJ will be able to forgive me, or any of us.'

His mind goes back to that night. The smells in the semi-darkness, flames flickering where their shack had been before: solid, protection, a home. His heart speeds up as he remembers trying not to panic. The taste of bile in the back of his throat. Telling himself to keep it together, for Maria, for the team. When all he wanted to do was retch and disappear, be anywhere but there. He was the leader, in a situation with no way out.

The woman he had loved died when he was making all those calls on the radio. He knows that now. But he still wishes he had secured that flight, more than anything he'd ever worked for in his life.

Lena doesn't say anything. She allows herself to be held, but she is holding back a bit of herself. Her hand stops the small caress she started, but she doesn't let go.

He feels her slip into sleep; he is amazed that she is able to, despite everything they have been through. But perhaps she isn't someone who dwells on the worries or should-haves, and instead just stores up energy for the day ahead. He kisses the top of her head, but she makes no move to acknowledge it.

He cannot sleep. He needs to figure a way out of this mess, for her, and for him. He needs to get them back to Malanje, back to safety and away from Carlos, away from this snarl of corruption. There has to be a way out; he just needs to think it through.

'Lena.' He gently shakes her awake before the sun comes up. 'We need to get out of here.'

The sky outside the window is a pale misty yellow, incubating the warmth of the day about to arrive. She takes a moment to remember where she is, and rubs a hand over her face and mouth.

'I don't think Carlos can just let us go back to Malanje,' he says. 'I'm really worried he will try to do something, and you could get hurt.'

'What about DJ?'

'I don't think she is here, do you? No one is here. Maria's family must have moved out a long time ago.'

'But the guards.' She looks out of the window.

'They never came back. Did you say you saw them smoking?'

'Maybe it was strong stuff.'

'If we move the bike, do you think you could stand on the seat and climb up over the fence?' He lifts his jacket off the floor, wrinkled from their weight.

The rain stopped in the night, but the water continues to flow down improvised channels towards the communal rooms. Their footsteps will easily be seen in the mud, but by the time anyone wakes up they could be far away.

Thirty-nine

London, 2000

Lena stood, partly sheltered from the rain by the overhanging gutters of the church. The air was saturated and her black dress puckered with the drops. She should have protected it. The shoes too – heels, almost never wore them – were marked with mud.

Behind her was the emergency exit. She tried to catch her breath, to compose herself before going back into the funeral. All those people, meaning well. Felt like strangers, most of them. How did they know her mother? What right did they have to take part in her personal grief?

The previous few weeks had passed in a fog. Lena had let tradition take over to mould the shape of the days since that phone call. The colleague from the hospital tried to phrase it kindly: Gloria had collapsed while on a break from her shift. She had had a heart attack and could not be revived. They did everything they could. At least she didn't suffer, the lady said in an automatic kind of way. Lena was forced to agree. Just like that, a heart gave up, a life ended.

Mum had been a long-serving member of the St Francis's Women's Committee, and they arranged everything about the burial and the Mass. The women correctly judged that Lena was too fragile to face those kinds of decisions – not now, maybe not ever. To do so would have taken a clear mind and strong belief. She had neither.

It took a while to get the message to DJ, who was on a field mission deep in Angola. They didn't know until just before the funeral whether she would actually be there or not.

Mum's sisters came from Lisbon, Aunt Eugenia and Aunt Euridice. They were shivering and smelling of fish and musty perfume, as they always had. People probably judged them, as their lipstick was too bright for the solemn occasion. They wore their diamond rings and wedding bands trapped between swollen knuckles, even though one had been widowed, the other divorced. But at least they came.

None of Dad's family were there. They had been in London eighteen months earlier for his funeral. As if some contract had been broken, this time they made their excuses or merely failed to respond.

She had stood by her mother's side after Dad's stroke. She remembered Mum's clasp of her hand, hurting-tight but it was all right. Lena, just twenty, felt that this was what she was there for. To be with Mum, greeting people and hearing the repetitions of banal things meant to be kind.

'So young,' they had said, each mentally comparing Eduardo's age to their own.

'God took him too soon,' wringing their hands, no longer knowing if a kiss on each cheek was appropriate.

The hugs, some deep and long. Others more of a pat on the back by someone afraid of the contagion of despair.

'You're so lucky to have the girls.'

Dad's coffin had been closed, as was tradition. That didn't stop DJ from dropping to her knees and wailing as if something inside of her had been lacerated. Lena had never seen her like that. DJ was always trying to contain sadness, declare it weaker than herself. Anger was her trademark. But here was a situation she hadn't prepared for. And it sliced her, as vicious and unjust as a knifing.

After her mother's death, Lena was in a daze. Her thoughts whirled in circuits. The last time she saw her mother, they were eating in mirrored silence over breakfast. Why did she run out of things to say? She should've tried harder. She didn't do enough to make her happy, after DJ moved abroad and Dad died. After the bank took the house and they needed to move into the little rental flat, just the two of them.

She knows now that she should have noticed that all the sunshine was already gone from Mum's face. Her skin had faded grey-pale. Forgotten were the lively makeup and curvy clothing that she used to wear to celebrate in daily life.

It's my fault, she thought. Why didn't I do more to cheer her, when I still had time? I have been so self-centred, only paying attention to Uni and photography. Thinking that there would be time, that all Mum needed was time. What a bloody fool I was. Missed so many chances. These loops repeated in her mind, leaving her raw.

Nice-sounding words from friends, colleagues and neighbours did nothing for the sadness. Some even wearing the same hats as they had for Eduardo's funeral. But something was wrong with her vision. Maybe the tears were getting caught in her eyelashes, but everything was blurred and a strain. She blinked too much and it irritated her. People only became clear when they came closer to her, and then it felt too close and she wanted to back away.

They murmured the same kinds of phrases as before, only managing to sound more pathetic this time.

'So sorry, my dear…'

'Too soon, God took her too soon…'

'Died of a broken heart, I'd expect.'

She couldn't speak, not very much. The 'how-are-yous' sent in her direction were well meant but meaningless. If she could have answered properly, she would have said that the overwhelming feeling was bitterness at being left alone.

The funeral packed the church, people crowding close to the coffin. Many faces were similar-aged women, lines around their mouths from decades of speaking a foreign tongue as they made their ways through a practical London working day. This was her mother's community. The place was filled to capacity with followers and friends who had walked with faith alongside her.

Lena was pinned to the centre of the front pew, with the aunties on one side, and the priest's sister Caroline on the other. They were crammed in so tight. Caroline seemed afraid that Lena might sway or topple, so she leaned in even closer with a hand to her elbow. There were hundreds of people, sitting calmly in pews, some gently weeping. The weight of expectancy pressed on her, as if there was a right way to believe and grieve, and she still didn't know how to do it properly.

DJ refused a seat and stayed towards the back. When Lena craned her head she couldn't see her through the pattern of faces and hats and heads, turning into silhouettes in the dim light.

Why couldn't DJ act like a normal sister, and be by her side? The thought clawed at Lena. That's what sisters do, for goodness sake.

As the priest spoke about Gloria and her work as a nurse, her involvement with the church and helping teen mothers, Lena recognised the public portrait. It was how her mother would have wanted it. There was dignity in that. But all the colour seemed to be missing. Where was the life-force that dominated the family?

What they weren't saying: about Mum's rising laughter – a bit too loud, as she teased Dad about his growing paunch. They weren't talking about her wide hips that swayed when she danced to music playing on the tiny radio in the kitchen while she finished the dishes. They weren't talking about how her voice rose in pitch and volume in an argument, never able to fully concede to the other point of view without losing face.

When the priest spoke about Gloria's calm presence of mind, Lena almost burst. That's not all Mum was! she wanted to call out. She was so much more. She had contradictions in her. Made you want to shout and argue a lot of the time.

Or those times when Mum had a look on her face when you spoke to her, as if her mind was partially somewhere else. Her children, once grown, were not enough to sustain her attention for very long. Maybe she hadn't planned on having us, wondered Lena. Maybe she just wanted to have her husband to herself and have a lively life in London together. Or maybe it was DJ, coming so soon after their marriage. Or perhaps it was the type of child DJ was, demanding and charged, that wore Mum down. Lena did her best to keep the peace, but it wasn't enough. She was never enough. Maybe she came too late, and Mum was already weary of it all.

She remembered that first photograph she ever took. It was a blurred one of Mum and Dad, leaning in to each other on the *Dia de Camões*, at the start of their annual party at the café. Dad had the scruff of a beard. He had experimented with the look until Mum told him no more kisses until it was gone. He shaved right away, didn't wait until the next morning.

Mum had such a strong sense of femininity, a purposefulness in it all. Not connected to being a mother, though, Lena realised with a jolt. But something even deeper, about being a woman, first. About the force of loving, and being loved.

Where had that gone? How could death snatch that away?

Lena's fingers, toes and hips tingled uncomfortably, needing movement. Her nerves felt angry, jumping around. She started to twitch and stifled a moan. Thoughts jumbled together, and for a moment she couldn't remember if it was her father's funeral or her mother's. She turned to ask her sister and realised it was Caroline at her side.

She restrained herself as long as she could, but the urge to stretch and move became impossible to ignore. She needed to reach out or hit the stained-glass windows and the cold sky outside.

Why was the priest still going on and on? What hope was there in repetition of Mum's story? Fake hopes, people telling themselves and each other what they wanted to hear: that life was meaningful, death couldn't cut that short. Bollocks. No words can change it, death takes it all away. She'd seen it before, when Dad died. Now with both of them gone, it felt like two columns of an archway had been demolished, like two swings of a wrecking ball coming through.

She couldn't take any more. 'Excuse me.' She pressed gently and then with more urgency to move past people. They looked concerned, but shifted to allow her to pass. They turned to look, but she couldn't stay in that place. 'Excuse me, sorry, must get some air...' Panic rose with a terrible taste in her throat. She was afraid she might vomit or shout or both. Mercifully she reached the end of the pew and half-ran towards a side exit. She didn't turn back to see who was looking, probably they all were.

The air was fresh and cold with the November rain. She heard the door click behind her and turned to see there was no handle on the outside. No matter. Let them shut her out, let it rain on her alone.

The rain smacked the leaves, those that had held on through into late autumn. Her breath clouded up into her vision and she shivered. She should go back in, she knew, but couldn't bring herself to.

'Want a fag?'

She turned to see DJ holding out a cigarette. She was wearing a black leather motorcycle jacket. Her hair fell into her eyes, blackened and wet, so she must have been out there awhile. It was a strange cut, long over her eyes but shaved shorter at the back, as if she'd done it herself or with a friend in front of a mirror.

'Didn't know you smoked,' Lena said, taking the cigarette.

'Could say the same for you.'

'Well you know, needs must.' Lena blew out and stifled a cough. She didn't smoke, not much, but sometimes there was no good reason not to. She moved to hand it back.

'No, you keep it,' DJ said. She looked out at the trees that outlined the square small garden behind the church. Autumn's colours were washed away into a smudge of browns and rotten black.

'All that Catholic bullshit about resurrection and purity of the soul,' DJ said. 'Mum didn't still go on about that, did she?'

She didn't reply. She thought DJ would know the answer, anyway.

'Well, it's not for me,' DJ added. 'But you're old enough to make your own choices, I reckon.'

'Everyone has their own way of making meaning from the pieces.'

DJ looked at her, as if she barely recognised her younger sister. 'What are you going to do?' she asked.

'It goes on for hours,' Lena said. 'After the burial, then there's a reception back at the flat. I'm not sure how long I'll stay. Caroline said I could crash at theirs if I couldn't face it.'

DJ looked away.

Lena felt a flush of a feeling she'd had throughout childhood – when she would say the wrong thing and immediately see that her sister had meant something entirely different. Could never quite fix it, somehow.

'What about you?' she asked. 'In London long?'

DJ shook her head. 'I have to get back. We're setting up new camps in the north of the country.'

'In Angola? Or somewhere else?'

'Still in Angola. It suits me.'

The door behind them opened. She heard Lucien's voice. 'You all right? Mass is over, you're safe now.'

She smiled, good old Lucien. But DJ stepped away.

'Wait,' Lena said. 'I need to talk to you—'

'Not here. I can't do it here, not while she is still here. She might be listening.'

It was an odd thing to say, but she was used to DJ saying odd things at times. 'Or we could catch up later? After the burial?'

DJ shook her head. 'You don't understand, do you?' she said, looking at a circle her boot was drawing in the muddy ground. 'Everything that woman stood for…'

Lena sensed the old anger surfacing from her sister, the way it always did. Why did she have to make a personal issue out of every occasion?

'You know, today of all days, couldn't you just try to… make peace with her?'

DJ grimaced and shook her head.

'Why don't you come round the flat later, collect some of your old things?'

No answer.

She tried again. 'Do you want any of Mum's belongings?

And her bank accounts or her pension, do you know about managing things like that?'

DJ flicked her cigarette to the ground and ground it in with the ball of her foot. 'I don't give a damn about that woman's things,' she said softly, as if she wanted to barely be heard. 'Do whatever the fuck you want.' Hands in her pockets, she rolled her lips flat and shrugged her shoulders.

'So that's it? You're just going to brush us off?' Lena was startled. She hadn't imagined doing this alone.

DJ looked at her with angry eyes, the whites lined with red.

Lena felt her own temper rise up from a trembling centre. She didn't want to make a scene, not now, not here. But she had spent a lifetime holding back and here was her own sister, giving Mum less consideration than a stranger would.

'You don't take responsibility for anything about this family, do you?' she burst out. 'You never did. Never fucking cared. You were off saving the world and doing whatever the hell you wanted. No time to conform to any cultural norms or, God forbid, anything we might need.'

'You don't have a clue about my life or what I do,' DJ shot back. 'I take responsibility every day. If I do a botched job on the water supply for a village, you know what happens? People die. Children die. Babies die, of a simple thing like diarrhoea. On a scale that makes individual losses just—' She stopped herself. Her arms had been lifting with the enthusiasm of her speech, but now they dropped to her side. 'Pale in comparison.'

'So what are you now? Some kind of engineer-saviour out there?'

'You never understood. She never got it either. That there might be some things more important than just her little domestic realm. She could never get beyond criticising the tiny details – how I looked, what I wore – none of that matters, don't you see? She was a tiny, narrow-minded woman. I'm not sad to see her go.'

'That's a really shitty thing to say about your own mother.'

'Yeah, well sometimes the truth is a bit shitty.'

'I can't believe you! On the day of her funeral, to be so self-absorbed that you can't even behave like a normal person. You should be fucking *grateful* to that woman who raised you, raised us. She had to have so much bloody patience to have you as a daughter, you have no idea what she put up with. You thought I was too young to understand but I would watch it all. You, coming storming in with whatever was the latest outrage. You always took up all the oxygen in the room. No one else could *breathe* with you around!'

She was nearly out of breath now with the force of her feelings. Today of all days, to have DJ insult Mum, was too much. 'Dad felt the same way too, you know. We all did. He just had more patience than a saint.'

She was surprised that DJ didn't have anything to say to stop her. She continued, 'Just fuck off to Angola then, if that's what you want to do. I hope I never see you again.'

Her sister looked at her with wide eyes, taking in the words without a buffer. She looked like her father in that moment; it was a gentle expression, almost smiling, that just gave a hint of the damage done. Then she turned and walked away across the churchyard.

As she was about to reach the boundary fence, Lena called out, 'DJ, no, sorry, I didn't mean it! I just...' But her sister disappeared out through a far gate.

Lucien came up behind her, offering her a coat. She let him put it over her shoulders, could not make the effort herself. She felt totally spent and used up.

Kind strangers swelled out of the church's main entrance and moved towards cars to drive to the burial. She knew she was expected to say certain things, move to the front, take a prominent role in the mourning. But she couldn't bear doing that.

It was no use. There was nothing left of the family, nothing to hold on to.

Forty

Lena stands on the wet leather seat of the bike, leaning against the gate. Don't slip, she tells herself. She puts one foot on a metal lock to hoist herself up higher. She feels the chink-noise all the way up to her jaw and clenched teeth.

'Keep going,' Kojo whispers.

She secures her next foothold and reaches up over the spike. Thank goodness it's not broken glass or barbed wire; it was a school after all, not meant to be a prison. She swings one leg between the spikes, moves her hips over and breathes out once she has cleared the other side, jumping down.

Taking a few steps forward, she looks up. Ahead of her the way is cottoned on all sides by mist blocking out the morning, soaking up the last of the storm's coolness. The road ahead is blank as the treetops over it blend into whiteness. Her heartbeat pounds in her throat. She wants to be absolutely anywhere but here.

After he lands on the ground, he senses her fear. 'It's all right,' he says, and takes her hand.

She can't tell if it's only her hand that is shaking, or whether his is too.

'Let's aim for the back roads,' he says.

'Do you think he'll come looking for us?'

He doesn't answer. He walks slightly ahead, pulling her forward.

She feels the sun's heat even before she can see it in the sky. It feels like yesterday's rains will evaporate quickly, and they will lose their cover before long.

The trees move in the early wind, birds cry out. But absent are the normal sounds of a village, even a sleepy one: no motors or generators, no dogs squabbling over the rubbish, no goats complaining. Where is everyone?

They walk, holding hands, saying nothing. She is afraid to look at her watch. She doesn't know what kind of man Carlos is. Will he let the two of them walk away, or will he come after them? How strong is the bond between Kojo and Carlos? Does it mean anything? Will it protect them? Or entrap them?

What if Carlos is holding DJ? Has he harmed her? She can't imagine DJ being held anywhere against her will. Her temper, her fury would drive others towards brinkmanship. No, she feels that her sister would not be held here. She doesn't know how she knows it, but she does.

'The nunnery,' she says.

He nods. 'But we need to take care of ourselves first. We're not out of danger yet.'

Kojo holds Lena's hand and adjusts his pace to hers. They are moving fast, but not fast enough. They have to get out of Luremo and onto the secondary roads. Those should still be cleared of landmines, but that remains to be proven.

Carlos, what have you established here? He wishes with all of his bones that he hadn't come, that he hadn't seen this: his friend descending into corruption and collusion with UNITA. He must have crafted it by design to suit his purposes. Total control of these young boys, as the villagers fled in fear. Free labour, paid in meagre amounts of food. Isolation from the MPLA hierarchies in the cities and the capital. Easy access to the Congolese border.

But what about UNITA? They used to control this area. Even though the conflict officially ended with the gunshots killing Savimbi, power here must have changed hands earlier. Some persuasion was needed, some deal struck. Carlos would have been good at that.

The mist to the east starts to burn into a pale orange as it prepares to greet the sun.

'We should run,' he says.

They drop hands and run together with matching strides. Lena tucks her hands up under the straps of her backpack to stop it bouncing against her body's rhythm.

She feels condensation on her forehead, nose, and upper lip. She can see the early sun balled up and powerful, yellow coming through the strands of the foliage that makes it clear that heat will prevail over yesterday's storm.

As she runs, her mind flicks through her memories like photographs – her mother, giving her the necklace that she passed to Benedito. Lucien finishing the forged visa letter. The look on Kojo's face when she first walked into the CWA office. Jeanette's hug engulfing her as she wept, just a couple of nights ago. The malnourished boys under armed guard, gulping down their food. The picture of DJ and Maria, tucked into her notebook.

The mist begins to lift, and she recognises that they have run out along the main road of the town. He points to a small road to the left. She knows she has no choice but to trust him. They need to keep going, get safe, and find DJ before the chance is lost. Too much is in motion to stop now.

But it doesn't feel right, leaving those boys behind. She can't shake off the image of them coming in last night. Silhouetted by the beams of the broken-down bus, exhaustion dripping from their shoulders. The way they struggled to hold their heads up. No one looking after them. Did they have no family? Had they been students at the school? Or child soldiers? There wasn't a chance to find out. That's the power of the gun, the potential to silence all lines of enquiry before they happen.

The side road turns a sharp bend and they are suddenly beyond the outskirts of the town. Buildings are less frequent, set back from the road. The bush is starting to close in again. The light becomes greener, filtered through the leaves.

She listens intensely for the sound of any cars or motorcycles that could be following them. If they hear anything, should she jump into the bushes, or not? He hasn't said whether he's concerned about landmines or booby traps here. Might be a split-second decision, depending on what presents the greater threat.

It seems as if the town is yet to wake up. She looks at her watch: 6.14 am.

When it is clear that Luremo is behind them, he slows down the run to a jog, then a walk. His breath is steady, as if he's been training for this kind of situation.

'Those boys,' she says.

'Slave labour.'

'Ex-UNITA?'

'Probably.'

'Shouldn't we have done something?'

He doesn't respond. She's learned that he's a man who, if he doesn't have the answer for something, says little.

'Do you think DJ knew?' she asks.

217

He pulls his lips tightly together and shakes his head. 'I think they would have said something. DJ would have had to do something. She has a strong sense of justice. She couldn't walk away from a situation like that.'

He stops for a second and pulls Lena closer. 'But that's why Maria was so good for her, you see? Maria understood people on a deep level. Even people committing terrible acts, she could understand them. Maria would have tried to protect those kids, if she had seen them. She didn't strike out against the power that held them. But maybe that's what got her, in the end.' He steps back, putting more space between them. 'I don't really know.'

She can't take her mind off Benedito, with no one to protect him. With people like Maria gone, who's going to help those kids now?

The sun rises high in the sky, and the mist burns away. She licks her lip and tastes salt. Her water bottle ran out a while ago.

He suggests they rest in a shady strip of land where there is a lightly trodden path peeling off the road. The path has been walked recently, but not since the rain. He moves slowly, gracefully, cautious. They can't stay on the road to rest. Just out of sight is a small clearing with some beaten-down grass. She sits down and slips her backpack off. Her shoulders are wet with sweat and feel cool now, exposed to the air.

'Today is Larium day,' she says.

'Do you have it?'

'No, forgot.'

'Ah well. No worries about the vivid dreams then.'

She smiles, thinking back to that time in her room before her mission here got more complicated.

'Do you have any water?' she asks.

He nods and lifts a spare bottle out of his bag. 'Go easy on it, we'll need it to last awhile. Unless we can find a safe way to collect the last of the rainwater.'

'I did remember the iodine,' she offers.

'We'll see if we need it.' After a pause he asks, 'Are you all right? Running in the heat?'

'I'm fine. It's better to be moving. We've got to get to DJ.'

Kojo whips his head around at the low sound of a large vehicle. It downshifts to brace against the hill in the last stretch of road. As the gears whine in protest, he judges it must be a heavy load. Silently, he pulls her head and shoulders down to a crouch in the side brush. They are as low to the ground as they can be, while still retaining the ability to spring up and run if they need to.

The vehicle finishes the bend in the road and he sees the top of it going past. It's a bus recycled from a previous lifetime. The paint is chipped and muddied, but you can still recognise that it served a mining company that used to operate across the border in Congo, now long gone bankrupt. The bus creeps forward at low speed, but the engine still screams at the effort.

'Head down,' he whispers. He prays to God they will not be seen. Hopefully the driver is distracted by the despairing engine and the state of the roads. He tries to wish away their parallel lines of footprints in the mud.

He feels her wobble, then put a knee down in the grass. He takes his hand off her shoulder – no need to restrain her, she would not do anything foolish. They look at each other and listen as the bus continues to groan forward but not far. The noise should be in the distance by now, but it is still quite close.

There is a squelch of brakes and then the mechanical exhale as the bus stops fully and snaps open the door.

'That's the bus from last night, isn't it?' she says.

He holds his fingers to his lips and tries to listen. They hear sounds of people descending the stairs, jumping to the ground. Clanks of metal, thumps of something duller like rubber. Other buses would have the chatter of children teasing or laughing, but not this one. Human communication is conspicuously absent.

After a while, the engine noise cuts out and all that's left is the swish of the bushes moving in the wind, and then silence.

Forty-one

Her legs begin to ache from crouching and she decides to stand up, startling him. 'It's okay,' she reassures him. He looks at her, worried.

But she knows. This part of the road isn't about her. There's another story here, one that has been neglected.

She tilts her head to indicate she wants to see what's going on. He shakes his head no. She wants to agree with him, stay back, be safe – but she can't. There's something not right.

She walks back to the roadside. The bus is parked about thirty metres ahead. There is no sign of the boys. The bush rounds off at that point and the road stretches out ahead into full sun. She runs slightly to see better.

Mounds of mud rise up in embankments on both sides with spiky long grass obstructing the view. She leans forward on the mounds and goes down to her elbows.

He whispers to her from a distance but she waves him away. 'Don't worry,' she whispers back. 'I just want to have a quick look.'

Before he can stop her, she starts to crawl on her hands and knees, hoping she blends in with the ground, the grass providing some protection.

In front of her is a slippery geometric landscape that is nothing like the bush or the dry high plains that she has grown familiar with since her arrival in Angola.

What on earth is this place? There is water everywhere, shiny and muddy, stagnant in places, fast-moving in others. Maybe an underground river has come to the surface? But it seems to have been altered beyond recognition. Spread out in all directions are choppy terraces, slanting into the riverbed. Along one side, the river runs fast, the water opaque from sediment. In the high banks next to it, like an amphitheatre, there are steps about one metre deep carved out from the surface of the land into the water table below.

The ledges are uneven and broken, sloughed off in places where mud must have collapsed in. Other steps break away from the fixed pattern to follow what might be smaller, haphazard branches of the river. Little pools have been dug, and all along each ledge and pool are dozens and dozens of children. It's the boys from last night. They blend in completely as they are covered in mud the same colour as the earth. They are wearing rags or oddly sized pieces of clothes or nothing at all. Most are barefoot, but some have flip-flops or broken shoes. One child is wearing a single boot.

They take no notice of her as they chisel with metal poles, sticks or anything straight. One digs with a spatula, another with what looks like a tablespoon that keeps on bending in his hand. They peer down into plastic bowls that are low and flat and helping them filter the muck. Some of the children are along the ledges, others are in the water, knee deep or waist deep.

She looks back towards Kojo. 'These are the kids!' she says, distressed.

'Lena!' he tries to whisper-shout. 'Get back! Someone will see you!'

She shakes her head. 'We have to do something, Kojo.' She crawls to the side, hoping she is staying out of view if there are any guards.

She watches the choreography playing out on all the different levels. The children are sifting, digging, shifting, scratching, and hoping for the sight of something. They are so exposed. No one's protecting them, and Carlos is probably profiting from all of this.

Without asking permission, she slips her camera out of her backpack and starts taking pictures. She balances on her elbows, and with her zoom lens she can get close. She wishes she had brought her digital camera, as this one needs to be reloaded every thirty-six shots. Please God don't let the mud get into the mechanism, this isn't the time for it to get jammed.

Framing each shot with a single decision then moving to the next, she has no time for extraneous thoughts. Her mind moves fast with the shutter, trying to best document this. There must be evidence. The scene cannot be allowed to be disappeared.

Some photos are of the wide landscape, the children just small figures at the mercy of something bigger. She takes several photos in a line, thinking about printing a panoramic view back in the darkroom later. Other shots are zoomed in – their facial expressions: grim and determined. Their arms: childlike, simple and strong, but angular and bony, lacking some essential nutrients. The squint of a child as something holds promise. Then a disappointed arc of a splash as a bowlful of water is thrown back in the mud, nothing found.

Her heart beats quickly. Her breath, let out in sighs, has a tendency to fog the viewfinder. Still, she keeps going. If DJ had known about this, she would have had to do something. Kojo said it – she had a strong sense of justice. But she's not DJ, not Maria. All she can do is bear witness.

She takes pictures of bodies half-buried in mud, yet the

children keep going. They seem to be forcing themselves in their rhythms that don't permit any variation. No time to wipe away sweat from their faces, or to clean their hands. Their determined searching continues despite the heat from above and the risks from standing in sludge for long periods of time.

She reloads the camera and shoots again and again.

Kojo does not know why he didn't manage to move more quickly, otherwise he would have stopped her before she came into the view of potentially anyone – so risky! Even on her hands and knees she could be seen. There now, she is sitting up and you can see her head above the grass. What the hell is she doing? Does she not realise? She could get them killed, for the love of God!

She crawls forward, and surprisingly fast she is out of his view. He can't let her go without him, so he too is pulled up over the mud mounds on his hands and knees, and sees the conflict diamond scene below.

It is bigger than he'd expected. He had heard about the warlords who forced villagers to scrape for diamonds, but he had imagined it being thin ledges on the banks of a river winding through the dry landscape. This operation is on a more industrial scale. Someone has calculated the most effective way to get a large number of labourers to sift through huge volumes of water and mud, and it is this: make it low, shallow, spread out, and use children who can't escape.

He watches Lena move to a new vantage point, wishing he had words to persuade her to stop. To tell her that she is endangering herself, most likely endangering the children too. What good will it do if she is killed and the photos are never seen?

She sees him. Near a ledge, on the far side, Benedito is holding an orange plastic tub that looks broken on one edge. It's much too big for him. He's struggling to keep it upright, full as it is with water and mud. A small kid, he looks like a survivor, precariously balanced. He walks quickly along the high banks of the river, a slick curve. He has no shoes and his feet are caked with fresh, wet mud. She holds her breath for him as he wobbles and nearly drops the tub, but he recovers before all is lost.

She gives a sigh of relief, and looks back at Kojo. 'He's there!' she says in a whisper-shout. 'Benedito's okay!' She turns back and takes a few more pictures, then stops to change the film again.

She hears a shout, and looks up to see the shape of the child slip over the bank into the waters below.

She screams out his name and jumps up. She tries to run towards where he fell, but there is a jigsaw of the paths, ledges and water in sunken holes. It is too convoluted, there is no direct route. She can't move fast enough.

When she reaches the bank, she can't see if he's surfaced or not. The water is cloudy and moving too fast. Where is he? Does he know how to swim?

'Oh my God…' She sees his orange tub a way downstream, caught in an eddy and spinning. There is no sign of the boy.

She drops to her knees in a violent move, nothing to protect her knee caps from the blow. Doesn't matter, just focus on the child. She prays to a God who may or may not be listening, every way she knows how.

'Oh God oh God, please save him, save this child, please! *Deus, por favor, meu Deus…*'

*

For a moment, it looks as if she is going to jump in as well. She would have, if she'd seen any sign of the boy. The current was probably too strong. She falls to her knees, defeated.

No one else seems to be reacting. Kojo's seen it before: when death is so common, comradery matters little. The kids keep sifting, moving mud, splashing it back.

He sees the armed men before she does. She is still shouting into the water for Benedito, does not realise or care that she is drawing attention to herself. They move quickly and yell and wave their guns to gesture her to move back from the edge.

The shouting finally pierces her awareness. She straightens up and stiffens her spine. Is she going to be hysterical or act professional? He can't guess.

She remains rigid for a second, then slowly gets up and turns around, palms up in surrender.

He could have left her there. Perhaps he should have. Could have crawled away into the bush and said no more. But he can't even consider it. Instead he comes out from behind the grass, running towards them with his hands in the air and shouting, 'We are a humanitarian mission! *Missão humanitária!*'

As the soldiers turn towards him, he sees the UNITA badge on their sleeves. Oh good Lord, he realises. These are soldiers who think they are still serving Savimbi. Who commands them now?

Forty-two

You fold the cotton trousers and shirts into tight squares, lined up with the edge of the bed. You wish you could say a proper thank you to Mama Iglese and all the other sisters who held you in this safe embrace for the past four weeks.

Or has it been more than that? You've lost track of time, those nights when you had fever. And the days. The early ones, when all you could do was watch the wall. And let regrets spill out over you in sobs and spit and tears.

Messy, degrading experience, sadness. You hate it. Not invited, never wanted, spreading to everything. But you have it now. It's with you and can't be cut away.

You can't say anything to the sisters. If they knew, they'd try to stop you.

You don't have a plan. Just an idea like a new breeze. Like a shift from the dry season to the rains. To the border. Start again, leave all this behind, forever. No explanations needed, because no explanation is possible.

Where to?

You unfold a map that you found in the abbess's desk. You remember how the name Lubumbashi used to make Maria laugh, her tongue rolling over the syllables. A scene you keep replaying in your head. Her beautiful round curves shaking up and down, white nightgown translucent in the dim candlelight. The web of the mosquito netting adding a soft layer to protect you both against the world.

She said she always wanted to see Lubumbashi, on the river Kafue.

She used to talk about a myth she heard growing up. A circle of women living together. They banished men in an attempt to keep war at bay. A collection of only women, living and loving, outside the reach of men. She called them *Abençoadas*, the blessed ones. In Maria's mind, they were holy and protected, linked somehow with the Virgin Mary, but no explanation was necessary.

You have to find them, these *Abençoadas*. To see if the story is real. Maybe once you find them you can leave all this behind. You'll shed your sadness like the top layer of skin coming off. Or you'll die trying.

Forty-three

Lena freezes with the soldiers' shouts.

'*Missão humanitária! Missão humanitária!*' Kojo calls out from behind as he dashes to meet her by the bank.

The soldiers also approach in a run. '*Jornalistas aqui não! Não autorizados!*'

It was the camera, of course. You couldn't see it any other way. No explanation would override that first impression. Not that she was trying to help people, help one child.

Where is Benedito? Did he make it? She can't afford to twist back and have another look. She prays that he made it out of the water, somehow, but she doesn't have any proof that God would listen to weak voices from a place such as this.

Fear of the soldiers overtakes her worry for the child. She frantically tries to think of what would be the best thing to do at this moment.

They slow down their run when it is clear that she and Kojo are not going to try to escape. Their uniforms are clean and free from holes. Patches on the arms show rank and merit. They all wear a square in the shape of UNITA's flag: red with a sun rising over a green-yellow landscape, animal silhouettes – a group declaring its connection with the land.

They keep shouting at her as they approach. Their faces are sweaty-angry and look like there's no possibility of negotiation. Are they going to shoot? Their words are a mixture of Portuguese and a local language, becoming less distinguishable as they get angrier, until they stop just in front of her.

One soldier, seeming to be the commander, reaches out and grabs at the camera strapped around her neck. She gasps as it jerks her head down, but the strap doesn't break. He jerks it again twice more, each time burning a line across her skin. As he moves to do it a fourth time, she says, '*Por favor*,' and moves slowly with both hands in concert to lift the strap of the camera over her head. Her hands shake as she holds it out to him.

He hesitates a moment. She can't read his eyes behind the sunglasses, but the mouth is stern, pulled down and square.

He knocks the camera out of her hands and towards the grey-brown water below. Without a noise, it is swallowed by the current. She holds back dismay and tries to keep her emotions under control.

He aims his gun directly at her. She can't take her eyes off that short distance from his trigger finger to her chest.

'We know Carlos!' she says suddenly. '*Sabemos Carlos!*' Does he control this place? Couldn't hurt at this point. Anything to distract them from the idea of shooting you now, of getting it over with. '*Carlos nos conhece! Pergunte a ele!*'

The four gunmen all jerk in surprise. The commander's mouth twitches and he does not lower his gun, but relaxes his hand slightly. The other three look to him for orders.

He pauses, then swivels around and uses the gun to point in the direction of a large building tucked behind a bend in the river, out of reach from the mud and the mining.

'*Leva eles la dentro*,' he orders. '*Amarrá-los.*'

Lena turns to Kojo, whispers, '*Amarrá-los?*'

'Tie them up,' he translates softly, as he holds his stance in a position of surrender.

The main soldier walks ahead of them, trusting his loyal followers to obey. On the back of his uniform are the letters *UNITA*.

Forty-four

Why, why did she have to tell them they know Carlos? It's not going to help. Innocent mistake, but oh how Kojo wishes they could take it back.

He sits, feet tied to a chair, hands around his back. The boys couldn't find any wire or string, so strips of ripped t-shirt hold him prisoner. He thinks he could probably pull free, if he didn't care about Lena next to him. And the gun pointing casually in his direction.

She is just out of reach. Tied the same. Side by side, a metre apart. They can see each other with peripheral glances only.

'*Ninguém fala*,' the commander said when they came in. No talking allowed. It is clear that he is the one the others defer to. His uniform looked pristine from a distance but up close sweat patches circle under the arms and his face has an oily sheen. He keeps his sunglasses on, even inside the warehouse with the dulled light. Kojo wonders if his eyes are bloodshot or not; that would say something about discipline.

Three of the five soldiers are boys. They have an aura of entitlement about them, as if they are controlled by their aspirations and hopes, rather than just fear. But intimidation would always be an element in these UNITA types anyway.

The methods they use are notoriously harsh. How else can they get those decades of allegiance? Kojo knows through the interviews CWA has done in the camps, talking to people seeking missing boys, fathers and uncles. He's heard stories of ritual rapes, executions and other violent rites of passage for the young boys. There is no going back for those who have committed atrocities under UNITA's command.

They are being held in a large building of tumbling down corrugated iron. Inside, the light from high-up broken windows falls onto the elements of an old factory. The machinery is stamped with the same logo as the buses, a Belgian company that long ago attempted to invest in this corner where Angola meets Congo. They didn't last long, but pieces of their enterprise have creaked on for years.

It is a surprisingly large space, probably once used for lorries. Accordion doors, ones that could have swallowed a whole fleet of deliveries, now only squeal open a crack to allow people through.

Kojo's mind is going through options, but none of them are ones he wants to choose. Rip through the ties? Kick off the legs of the chair? Take on these guys? Not conceivable while guns are trained on him, and Lena is there. Can't let anything happen to her, not now.

He has been in difficult situations before, working in Loki negotiating with the Sudanese militias, and that time of the armed robbery of the warehouse in Luanda. But this is different. After tying them up, the commander and his underlings have left them with a sole gunman. He has a choice of who to shoot first, Kojo, or the woman Kojo has started to care about.

Kojo can't let that happen. There has to be a way out. His training in hostage situations comes to his mind, as he flips to that page in the script.

233

Remind them of your humanity. Connect with the man. He does what he always has done. He gets the guy to talk.

She tries not to think of Benedito. Just a child. That sweet child. The round cheeks on top of that body with those impossibly skinny legs. Could God have heard her prayers? She thinks of her mother's St Christopher around the boy's neck. Is there any chance he got out of that river?

But she has to think about herself now, and Kojo. Fucking hell, where are they?

Looking around, she sees frightening shapes and shadows that she doesn't recognise from any familiar landscape. The light is hazy-grey and obstructed by dust in the air. Odd threatening forms jut out in spirals, cranks and levers. It might be an old factory. She can't imagine what the machines were used for, although there is a strong smell of chemicals. It seems like nothing has served its normal function in years, perhaps decades. What do they do in this place?

Sweat runs down her jawline and irritates her ear. She tries to wipe it away with her shoulder, but the movement invites a nasty glance from the gunman. Perspiration gathers between her breasts, hidden by her shirt but still making her feel exposed. She feels it collecting between her trousers and her seat and she shifts – hopefully too subtle to notice – in the chair.

'*Não*,' the guard says with a growl. '*Não mexe.*' He is the only one of the UNITA guys not wearing sunglasses, an older guy left behind to guard them when the others were called away. One of his eyes is clouded with grey, the other is clear and jerks around the room constantly. It is not clear what he is looking out for, but it seems to be something he considers an ongoing threat.

After a few minutes, he settles down and then his face seems to glaze over into a distant, calmer expression.

The place smells of iron and other metals, stagnant water and dust, and something turgid and menacing that she cannot name. Also smoke, herbal and spicy. She's not sure if it's marijuana or something more potent. Opium?

Her mouth is so dry that the corners hurt. She'd asked for water, but was ignored. The men ignore everything she says, after the Carlos comment. It was as if she had somehow invited a higher power into the conversation, and soon she would no longer be their problem to deal with.

Is Carlos a threat, or the chance for a reward for these men? Then where will she and Kojo be when it comes to that? Carlos won't be happy to see them. He would probably like to see them disappear, like Maria, then DJ.

What would DJ do, if she was here instead of Lena? Rage against the bindings? And get shot?

She thinks back to the times in childhood, when DJ would square up to a bully. Sometimes she would get knocked back, if she chose someone rough or older. Other times she had this thing where she would say her piece and then sprint away, running faster than they could realise the meaning of what was said.

She'd come home, with a black eye or scrapes, but with self-assuredness intact. DJ always had a sense of justice, and put herself on the side of the just. Every time, somehow, she could argue it that way.

Lena remembers her mother washing away blood and dirt from DJ's face in the bathroom sink. Gently trying to press her elder daughter to consider the alternatives to fighting. DJ shaking her head, arguing still, but the energy gone. The blood-pumping excitement of defending yourself, defending the family or anyone, dissipated out and went down the drain with the blood and the day's dirt.

Lena would sit on the top of the closed toilet seat. A silent observer, trying to figure out who to learn from: the fighter, or the healer? Both had power, used it very differently. And neither one could be anything else, could comprehend anything else. Lena saw both, listened to both, grew up with both, and had them entwined inside her.

'How long have you been based here?' Kojo asks in Portuguese.

Cloudy-Eye brings himself back from his thoughts, pausing before deciding to answer. 'Fuck off,' he says.

Kojo nods and sits back in the chair. 'Fair enough,' he says. He thinks a moment. 'I would probably say the same thing if I had to work under a gun like you.'

Cloudy-Eye makes a face like a bad taste on his tongue. 'What the hell do you mean? I don't have a gun pointed at me. That's you, motherfucker.'

'Right. In your hands. And yet, what if you were free to go?'

'I am free.'

'Course you are. But if you were really free, is this what you'd be doing? Hanging out with me and my lady friend here in this shithole?'

'Shut up! My grandfather built this place! You don't know what the fuck you're talking about!'

Kojo pauses. Has he judged this man wrong? He lets the anger simmer down for a few minutes.

There's a steady rumble of a generator outside, from another building that outranks this one. Here, no air conditioning. The overhead fans are stuck in time by cobwebs.

After a while, he tries again. 'You're from here?' he asks.

He gets a sharp short nod in response. 'What brigade are you with?'

'Luremo Manor, Thirteenth Brigade.' A certain amount of satisfaction comes with this allegiance.

'I've heard of the Thirteenth. Weren't you in that siege in Caxito?'

Cloudy-Eye sits up a bit taller, looking proud. 'Where we slaughtered the government's forces, you mean.'

'Outnumbered and outflanked, yet you were victorious. People still talk about it.'

This gets a half-smile from Cloudy-Eye. 'And then we've been stationed here, defending the territory from the MPLA and the collaborators.' He pins his good eye on Kojo, as if daring him to prove he was not a traitor himself.

'Are you getting ready for disarmament?' Kojo asks.

Cloudy-Eye narrows his eyes with distrust.

'You know, with Savimbi's death,' Kojo continues.

He spits to one side of Kojo's shoe. 'A hoax,' he says.

'You think so?'

'Propaganda, nothing more. He's in hiding. The leaders will bring him out again when the time is right.'

'What do you do until then?'

'The usual.'

He pauses, trying to sense what holds this man to his post. Thinking through what might work with the man who threatens him and Lena beside him. Without a direct attack, the fault needs to come from within. From doubt.

'My brother,' he says. 'You are fighting for a dead man.'

'He's not dead, I tell you!' Cloudy-Eye raises his voice, but doesn't shift his body language from its settled place in the chair.

'No man is immortal. He was definitely wounded, even

UNITA says so. But we all are dying, anyway, are we not? In this war. Dying, slowly dying.'

Cloudy-Eye doesn't disagree. He moves his mouth around like there's a taste he doesn't like and can't get rid of.

'What's your name, my brother?' he asks.

Cloudy-Eye hesitates, then gives in: 'Francisco.'

'Francisco. I like the name. A trustworthy name.'

He grunts.

'My brother, what if the war was over, and you could just walk away? Go home again?'

Francisco looks away from him, at the machines in the large factory hall.

'Go back, change what was done, make it new again?' he continues.

'What do you know?' Francisco shouts, standing up. He swings his gun around with one hand, the other gesturing wildly. 'You fucking West Africans, coming in here! You're all just in it for the money, then you head out again.

'This is my home,' he says, more softly now. 'It looked different, once. My grandfather, he bought this equipment from Belgium. My father and uncles put the machines together. They couldn't read French but used their hands and worked it out.

'Come, do you want to see?' He reaches to untie Kojo's leg bindings. He turns to Lena. 'Not you,' he says sharply. 'You wouldn't understand.'

Francisco leaves Kojo's hands bound behind his back, but unties the legs. He motions for him to stand up. Kojo moves slowly, making sure that Francisco feels in control.

'It was beautiful, in those days,' Francisco says, walking towards the orderly rows of dusty machines. 'The equipment shone in the sunshine and made such a noise you couldn't think straight. You felt like it was progress, that we'd all be rich soon. I was here as a small boy.'

Kojo doesn't dare look at Lena as he gives the appearance of full attention to the man. In his peripheral vision he scans the corners of the room, trying to think through an escape plan.

'See this one?' Francisco continues. 'This was for taking the iron out of the soil. First it went in this conveyor.' He motions for Kojo to come to the other side of the machine. 'Then the magnets sensed the iron and pulled it out of the mud, even small bits of dust. Iron was a big industry back then, we supplied all sorts of places – Congo-Brazzaville, Kenya, Japan. All from here.'

Kojo nods and maintains eye contact at key moments in Francisco's sentences, but he is focused on the ideas rolling around in his head.

Could he kick the gun out of his hands? Could he work his own hands free without Francisco realising?

'I was young but I was given the job of oiling the moving parts. They would turn them off once an hour, and there I would be with the machine oil.' Francisco's good eye focuses on something far away, but then his face changes emotion.

'And then the elites in Luanda attacked this and shut it all down. My grandfather, his blood is in this factory, in the floor and the earth all around. They took away our means of production, trapped us by landmines and we could no longer reach the markets.

'But UNITA here, they didn't abandon us. They fought with us, against the Russians and the Cubans and other opportunists. UNITA stayed. Now we have another business. We'll find the diamonds, and one day we'll be so lucky we won't need any of this any more.'

'What if you don't need it already, now?' Kojo says. 'My friend, UNITA has laid down their arms, I tell you. Anyone who says differently is lying to you, in order to keep you working for them. Keeping you from being free. For this – the diamond mining, the children slaving away outside – all of this set-up is about to come tumbling down.'

Francisco's face twitches. He looks as if he already believes Kojo, but has to keep up appearances.

Does he have any power after all, other than holding a gun over two strangers?

Lena sees the accordion door move before they do. She tries to leap to her feet but has forgotten that she is tied to the chair. Her body jerks back and the chair scrapes its metal legs on the concrete floor with a terrible screech that makes Francisco spin to point the gun at her.

Kojo looks quickly at her, then swivels to see what made her jump.

The UNITA commander steps in first, followed by Carlos and two other armed men. They walk closely together, as if to defend their leader against any threats.

Carlos's face shows little emotion when he sees Kojo and Lena. It's as if he is already tired of thinking about them, or of failing to decide what to do with them.

Forty-five

'So, this is where you thought you'd find the runaway DJ?' Carlos says, looking from Kojo to Lena.

Kojo examines Carlos's face. He looks worn, as if he's been working long and it hasn't yet paid off. He has more lines on his face than a lot of Angolans. Why did he never see that before? Probably there's a lot of history that Carlos hasn't shared. He rarely reveals information, keeps it hidden unless it's useful to share. Kojo only knows about the landmine accident because he was there that night.

'I hope you were comfortable at the school,' Carlos says as he steps closer to where Lena is restrained. 'Shame about the storm.'

Everyone is still, watching him.

'Come, my friend.' Carlos pulls up another folding chair next to Kojo's empty one. With difficulty, he straddles the back of the seat. He pats the seat that Kojo left behind.

'I'd rather stand, thank you very much,' Kojo says.

'No, please sit, my friend,' Carlos says.

Kojo doesn't move.

Carlos looks at Francisco, and the other armed men. 'Kojo, my friend, please sit. See, I'll ask my men to withdraw.' He gestures for them to go, including Francisco. 'But leave me a gun,' he says to the commander.

The commander hesitates, before lifting his machine gun off his shoulder strap and walking it over to Carlos.

'Not that one. *A pistola, por favor.*'

The commander rests his machine gun against the wall, within reach of Carlos. Then he takes a handgun, concealed inside his belt, flips over the handle and holds it out to him. Carlos nods for the four of them to go.

After the accordion door is pulled shut, the faint wind settles down and a sour metal smell dominates. He sets the handgun in his lap, and takes out a cigarette and a lighter.

'Hate this place,' he says, looking at the flame. 'Stinks like shit.' He looks at Kojo. 'Want one now?'

Kojo raises his shoulders in a gesture to show that his hands are still bound.

'I see,' Carlos says. He looks at Lena, distrustful, then back at him. 'If you will take a cigarette, I'll untie you so we can sit properly together, like men.'

Lena watches Carlos swing his leg once again from the chair. He is not graceful. The two sides of his body are always a bit out of sync and unbalanced. That's what a landmine accident will do, and he was lucky to survive.

Carlos puts the lit cigarette between his teeth as he unties Kojo's hands. 'There,' he says. 'Now, please, join me.'

Kojo turns the chair and mirrors Carlos, facing him directly. This makes Carlos turn away from Lena, removing her from the man's line of sight.

Sweat is beading on Kojo's forehead and rolls to his temple, but he doesn't wipe it away. He is fully focused on Carlos.

The factory air is still and dry. She feels like she is inhaling tiny particles with every breath. She pulls with small movements at her wrist bindings. The t-shirt material is soft and weak. She thinks of the rags the children were wearing, worked to threads and worn through. She starts to stretch the material and gains some length.

'I never thought this war would end,' says Carlos. 'Did you?' He holds the pack out to Kojo, who takes one and leans forward for it to be lit.

'Of course, there were rumours in the weeks before,' Carlos continues. 'The bastard was so corrupt, I'm surprised it didn't happen earlier. But I don't suppose we'll ever know the full story.'

Kojo shakes his head no, slight moves with no enthusiasm.

'So...' Carlos flicks off some ash. 'What are we going to do with you two?' He exhales the smoke in a sigh. 'I tried to make you turn back, you see. But you didn't listen.'

Kojo's eyes remain fixed on Carlos, not risking a glance to her.

'And then instead of going home, you come here and try to take pictures? What do you want to do, get shot?'

Kojo takes a few drags on the cigarette as he composes his words. 'That wasn't the plan,' he says slowly.

'Let me tell you my plan,' Carlos says, leaning his shoulders forward into the chair. 'To finish all this, get the main operation over the border within a week. The diamonds with me. The boys, we'll take care of. The others, the leaders and the older ones, they come with me into Congo. We reward them for their loyalty.'

Her breath goes fast and shallow. Take care of the boys? What does that mean?

'This,' Carlos gestures to the factory's twisted rusting shapes around him, 'all this is useless, and stays rotting in place. The triumphant Republic of Angola can have all this shit.

243

'Then, you see, you humanitarians will be happy. The area will be cleared of rebel fighters and dangerous elements. People can start returning. Donors will pay for supplies. Demining can start. Villages can come back. Peace restored. That's what you want, right?'

Kojo nods with only a small movement. His mouth holds tight and silent.

'So there's no need to report this transition time, is there?' Carlos says. 'It's transitory, going to move on very soon. Hardly worth any notice at all.'

His shoulders roll back as he takes a deeper breath. 'Kojo, we've been friends for years. You always could see things clearly. It doesn't do to stir up things and bring reporters around.' Carlos turns his head around to see Lena. 'I'm surprised that you didn't show more sense.' The gold tooth that she first saw back at the police station reveals itself in a cynical smile alongside a range of greying teeth.

Kojo tenses his whole upper body when Carlos looks at her, but then lowers his shoulders back down. He'll be trying to maintain calm, but she knows his mind is racing. Trying to make a plan to get out of here, and quick.

Carlos turns back to Kojo, while she recommences trying to stretch the t-shirt fabric around her wrists.

'Kojo – you, I could let free. I can trust you. We go way back, you and me. I know what kind of a man you are. One who knows how to keep his word. Head down, in order to get the work done. That's what you've always done, isn't that so?'

'The work is important,' Kojo says.

'But why bring a journalist here? That was the wrong move, my man.'

She slips one hand out of the bindings.

'Asking questions, taking photos,' Carlos continues. 'Wrong place, wrong time.'

Kojo leans forward. 'What's the deal now, Carlos?'

'You get to go back to helping people,' Carlos says.

'And Lena?'

She swallows and feels like the whole factory can hear her gulp.

'Can't have witnesses,' Carlos says slowly.

'You can't just make her disappear,' Kojo says. 'People would notice.'

Carlos takes another drag from the cigarette.

'She's got connections in the embassy, and in London,' Kojo continues.

Carlos doesn't answer.

'People would talk,' Kojo presses him. 'It could get really messy for you.'

Carlos takes his cigarette away from his lips and lets ash fall on the floor. 'I've done it before,' he says.

She feels stretch enough in the bindings to twist her other hand free. She betrays no emotion in case he glances round again.

'Maria,' Kojo says in an exhale.

Carlos takes his time to reply. 'Sometimes people return to old places with new eyes, see too much.'

'But she understood. She was local. You said it yourself. You said she was the kindest person you'd ever met.'

'She was,' Carlos says. She can hear regret in his voice.

'You could have trusted her,' Kojo says.

Carlos blows a shaft of smoke that goes up above his oiled hair, dissipating towards the rafters.

Carlos set the explosion. Her suspicions are confirmed. Did Kojo know? The look on his face – surprised, shocked and damaged by Carlos's actions – says no. He's hurt by Carlos's recklessness, more deeply, more personally than you'd think.

'It wasn't supposed to be Maria, was it?' she says.

Carlos twists his chair around so he can see her. His cheekbones are prominent with hollowed gaps underneath. She can tell that he was handsome once. But she thinks of Benedito and the boys and hates him all over again. She hopes she is holding her hands convincingly as if they are still bound.

'What do you know?' Carlos growls.

'Doesn't take a lot to figure that while everyone was a bit in love with Maria, DJ didn't quite have the same effect,' she says. 'Rubbed some people up the wrong way, maybe? As you said. Her temper, her lifestyle, a bit different?'

Carlos frowns, looking at neither her nor Kojo, but ahead at the machines petrified in rust.

'That's why everyone is reeling, as the wrong person was killed,' she says.

Kojo's eyes narrow in on Carlos's face. The bastard responsible for Maria's death.

'You could trust Maria,' Carlos says. 'She and DJ saw too much, knew too much. Their clinic was at the wrong time, just when we were clearing Luremo. But Maria, bless her, you could talk to her. You'd believe her when she promised not to say anything. She knew what was good for her. But DJ, that woman–masquerading–as–a–man, you didn't know. He had a fire in him. You're his sister, you should know. I couldn't trust him to just let us finish the business.'

Kojo's heart is pounding. He wishes the bastard would stop talking but Carlos keeps going.

'The diamond mining doesn't last forever. Each site dwindles down eventually. It's not profitable to keep it going. It would only have been a few more weeks. Soon we will be over the border. Luremo will open up again for people to return.

'But DJ, he invited that FCO guy here to file a report. Wrong move, too much exposure. It could have jeopardised the whole operation.'

'What made you think—' Kojo says, but Carlos doesn't let him interrupt.

'I saw them together, man. With my own eyes. They were not even hiding it. They were actually out in the open, meeting in our Thursday-night bar. Our place, man! And having a loud, angry conversation. Everyone could hear. Obviously very passionate about things, talking about making a breakthrough. Can't you see how that challenges my authority here, talking like that on my own turf? I couldn't just let it go. The boys are watching me, seeing if there's any chance to bring me down. MPLA, UNITA, they would be only too happy to topple the man on top if there was any weakness showing.

'What could I do, man? I couldn't just let all my hard work get exposed, right before it was about to pay off.' Carlos turns to look at directly at him. 'You know what I mean, brother? I had to do my best before my chance was gone. Anyone would do the same I did, given the timing. Seize their opportunity.'

Without warning Lena drops her hand-ties and lunges at the machine gun leaning against the wall. Her chair screeches on the concrete as her legs are still tied. She manages to reach the gun and it clatters to the ground. She drops to her knees and scrambles to get a hold of it.

Carlos shouts, 'Stop! Goddammit!' He tries to leap up as well but his legs are tangled in his chair and it smashes to the floor.

Kojo dives for the handgun just as it falls off Carlos's lap onto the ground.

'Freeze!' Kojo shouts. Carlos looks at her, then him, calculating which is the bigger threat.

Kojo holds the handgun as if he knows exactly what to do with it.

'Take it easy, my man,' Carlos says.

Kojo's breathing is heavy and the flush of blood racing around his skull drowns out Carlos's voice.

'Freeze!' he shouts again.

His arms are solid, no shaking to betray his fears.

'Hang on, brother, you wouldn't shoot an old friend, would you?' Carlos has both hands palms up.

Kojo is fixed like a statue, arms in a triangle pointing directly at Carlos's chest. He can't move. Wants everyone to just stand still for a moment while he figures out what the hell to do, how to get the fuck out of this.

'You're a humanitarian,' Carlos continues. 'You're all about saving lives, right?'

'Shut up!' he says. Spit falls from his lips and he doesn't care.

'We go way back, my man.' Carlos moves a small step closer. 'I would never hurt you, bet my life on it.'

'Shut the fuck up!' he says. 'All of this! It's got to stop! I need to think!'

His legs tremble, making him feel like he is about to lose his whole foundation.

'You wouldn't... you couldn't...'

He can't pull the trigger.

She sees him hesitate, and she knows. He cannot kill a man. It would be like killing a piece of himself, his honour and his truth.

She struggles with the gun in her hands. It is much heavier

than she'd imagined. On her knees it's hard to shift the weight to her advantage. It's pointing far too high.

Her mind comes back to the boys, and Carlos's threat to take care of them before he runs for the border. This is a man who treats children as disposable. He killed Maria. And DJ – the real target of his operations – is on the run.

She remembers the child soldiers who have held these same weapons out in front of her, making demands, keeping her still.

If they can do it, why can't she?

The men are locked eye-to-eye, unable to resolve.

He's got to stop. Someone has to stop this man.

She braces the gun against her ribcage, aims lower, at Carlos's good leg, and squeezes.

Part V

Forty-six

Rain pounded at the windows. Gloria's forehead creased with worry as she squinted to try to see if the girls were on their way in.

With a bang, DJ burst into the café. She flicked her short hair both ways to shake off the rain. Like a dog, Gloria thought. My daughter, the puppy.

Gloria pulled her foot out of Eduardo's soothing rub and placed it back in her nurse's shoe. Before jumping to criticise, she looked, really looked at the fourteen year old in front of her.

She stands like a boy, Gloria realised. The stance is wide and confident. Her shoulders are broad as if she hopes for generosity from the world. But then she hunches a bit, as if expecting a scolding.

There were streaks of wet mud up to her knees. She must have splashed through puddles to show her power. Her exuberance at the world physical was ever present. The craving for fresh air, the cartwheels in the rain. Her total lack of regard for the feminine side of the world, with its own healing energy and light. Her daughter, destined to be a man and miss out on it all.

Gloria didn't like the thought. She couldn't help frowning. Why couldn't DJ be more like her? Why couldn't she see the power and beauty of being a woman? Why has she turned her back on her mother, of all people?

But she knew, even as she argued with herself: DJ couldn't change. She was who she was. She was going to struggle wherever she went. And the world being what it was, she would have to keep running. One step ahead at all times, to outrun those against her.

She failed to remember how she herself was, as a teenager. That she had a similar feisty, sometimes angry rhythm that could set people off against her. That she was bursting to escape the rituals and patterns of the family she was born into. Distance and time had blurred these forgotten memories, assumed to be unimportant now.

She wanted to reach out and hold this child close to her breast one more time, as if it wasn't too late. But then she remembered the rain and the mud and the last arguments they'd had, and she pulled back.

'Where is your sister?' she asked sharply. 'Did you leave her out there in the storm?'

DJ's look of triumph fell as her eyes darted back to the outside. It was clear she had forgotten Lena.

'She's six, for Christ's sake!' Eduardo leapt up and grabbed his raincoat from the peg. 'She follows you everywhere, worships the ground you walk on. And you just abandon her?' Swinging the door open he shouted back at DJ, 'Where did you last see her?'

Before DJ could reply, Lena was at the doorstep, sodden and solemn. Through sobs she said she found her own way home from the car park where the kids liked to play on rainy days. She was saying something about a bicycle, not making a lot of sense. It was clear that DJ had forgotten all about her responsibilities to her sister. No maternal instinct at all, that child.

Eduardo scooped Lena up and rubbed her with the lining of his raincoat. 'Come eat a *pastelaria*, my little mouse,' he said. 'Let's warm you up from the inside.'

DJ watched her father move behind the pastry counter. She had a look on her face like she was trying to figure out where she went wrong, but was missing some crucial insight. She wore that look a lot, one that blended unease with a growing sense of injustice, objecting to her treatment by the world.

When DJ looked up again, Gloria could not meet her daughter's eye.

Forty-seven

His friend screams out in shock and pain. But this time, Kojo steps around him and focuses on helping someone else.

She was knocked back by the firing. The look on her face is like she didn't think she could do it. As if she is wondering who it was who pulled the trigger, who she has become.

He thrusts the handgun into his pocket to get it out of his hands. They untie her feet as fast as they can go. He shields his eyes from seeing Carlos on the ground, howling.

'Sorry man, really sorry,' is all he can say as he grabs her hand and they run out of the door.

Where are the guards? Did they hear what happened? Will they come running, or are they too high to notice?

No one is outside the accordion doorway. She pulls him behind the side of the building, so they are not exposed to the mining site, and they run towards the bush.

'*Para!*' A shout comes from behind them.

They stop and put their hands in the air, turning around to see who threatens them.

Francisco stands about twenty metres away. He is in the stance of a soldier and his weapon is aimed at them.

'I could have shot you,' he says in Portuguese.

'I know, brother,' says Kojo.

'I should shoot you.' He rolls his tongue over his top teeth while he thinks about it. 'Shoot you both.'

After a pause, Kojo says, 'But maybe you won't?'

He lifts his chin. 'No?'

'Maybe you'll see that it does no good.'

Francisco grunts.

'Doesn't help anybody, doesn't help you.'

'What do you know?'

'I know you want to get back to your business, your life. This war is over. This will be over soon and you'll want to forget all about it.'

'You don't say.'

'You're a good man, Francisco.'

The silence feels thick with only a slight breeze moving the blades of spiky grass at the margins of the mining site.

'Let us go, my friend.'

Only the slightest nod comes from Francisco, but he does not lower his gun.

Kojo very slowly reaches for her hand. He makes large movements, easy to read. He turns to walk, then starts to run in the opposite direction.

The gun goes off, aimed just above their heads. They duck on instinct but do not look back. They do not stop.

'The bush,' she says, and leads him towards the protection of the trees. Her face is streaked with sweat and the industrial dirt of the place. She is beautiful in that moment, lean and strong.

The handgun bounces against his thigh. He hates it so much it feels like it could burn him by its touch. He rips it out of his pocket and throws it in a high arc deep into the trees.

Then he runs. Like everything up until now was just a rehearsal for the real thing.

Night is falling when they reach the nunnery. She has thought about this place, more and more in the recent days. What would it be like, this sanctuary?

Turns out it is nothing more than a dirt driveway smelling of old wood and chickens. An uncomplicated building with doors in a straight line, and a square communal hall with the smell of cooking rising out of it. That's all. It's painted with care, in a bright white that shows the efforts of the believers. A large crucifix hangs above the door, looming over their heads as they knock.

'They won't follow us here,' he says. 'It's kind of a protected space. After the Catholic mission treated both UNITA and MPLA soldiers alike, the local church demanded that this space be declared neutral territory.' He points to a sticker fixed to the window pane. 'See, no guns allowed.'

'And they respect that?'

'Most of the time, maybe. We have to trust.'

The woman who opens the door is stooped over so much that, even with a cane for support, she only comes up to Lena's shoulder. Her face is lined and double-lined with decades of survival and belief knitted together. She moves very slowly and says nothing, but she appears to know Kojo. She gestures them inside and hands them a leaflet. It says in Portuguese that the nunnery is open to visitors, but is under a vow of silence for Lent. Any understanding believer is welcome to stay in a simple room and share meals for a small donation.

He gestures that they would like two rooms. The nun nods, steps away from the door for a minute. When she returns she holds two room keys and two bundles of towels, sheets and clothing.

The shower is not warm, but it is exactly what her skin wants. The cold water makes her feel awake and purposeful. The only light comes from up high, a cut in the concrete shaped like a crucifix.

She wraps herself in a towel and walks back to her room. On her bed is a clean pair of cotton trousers and a simple shirt. The kindness of strangers, taking care. It makes her want to weep.

There is a knock at the door, and she hears Kojo's voice. Without thinking, she opens the door and gestures him inside. She suddenly feels self-conscious in her towel, her skin not yet dry underneath.

'You clean?' he says.

'I tried,' she said. 'Some things don't scrub off too easily.'

He is smiling at her, and she can't hold back either. He too has had a wash and is wearing a larger pair of the clean white loose trousers and shirt. He looks relaxed as she's never seen him. She is struck by how handsome he is, when he smiles.

'You have a bruise,' he says, looking at her knees.

She pulls them both together. 'Matching ones,' she says, looking at the blue–green patches. 'But they'll heal I suppose.'

'I'm sorry about your camera,' he says.

'That's all right. I have the other one back in Malanje, remember? The digital one.'

'For family tracing.'

'Or something like that. And look there.' She points to the bedside table. On it are three rolls of film.

'You managed to save something?'

'They didn't check my pockets. We lost the camera, but we still have most of the evidence, if we need it.'

'Let's see what we can do with it. I'll have a think who I know working the news wires.'

'There was a letter,' he says. 'For us.'

'Us?'

'Read it. The nuns gave it to me just now.'

She folds her towel tighter over her breasts and sits down on the edge of the bed with crossed legs. It is firm, a thin mattress over wood.

The envelope is addressed to CWA Malanje, in DJ's handwriting. It is torn open. The letter is short, and the handwriting is messy like it was written in a hurry.

28 February 2002

Dear Kojo, Jeanette and Brad,

It is with sadness that I hereby tender my resignation from CWA. There, that's the formal bit. You know I love you guys, but now it's time for me to move on.

Kojo – you've been the best boss I've ever had. You won't believe me but it's true. Here's hoping that some day I'll see you finally crack a smile in that serious face of yours.

Brad – I'll never forget your terrible American accent and your ability to wield a pipe under duress. Have my Coldplay CD, I wasn't that into them anyway. Actually, you can have my whole CD collection. Maybe you'll learn something about taste in music.

Jeanette – sorry, but I never will like The Cranberries. Their music is just too airy-fairy. Forgive me. But I'll miss you my dear, you're one of the best. You and Maria were brilliant to see in action, working together.

You guys have been like family to me, there's no other way to say it.

Speaking of family, please get in touch with my kid sister, Mags (Magdalena). Last I heard she was still trying to make it as a photographer and had never managed to leave London. I think you can reach her c/o her old sweetheart Lucien Franks at 41 Wilberforce House, Brixton Road, London, SW9, something. I don't know the rest of the postcode but someone in the embassy can probably look it up for you.

Please could you send her my journals and photographs, she'll get a kick out of those. And tell her I'm sorry I've been away so long. I missed most of her growing up, but I do love her in my own way. I hope to see her before too long down the road.

You are amazing, never forget that what you do here is vitally important.

Stay well, you blessed people,

DJ

'What do you think?' he asks.

'It's not long.'

'Goodbyes don't have to be.'

'She was here? It's today's date.'

'Left this morning, I think. By motorcycle.'

'So we're not far away! We could probably catch her tomorrow, what do you think?'

'Does she want to be found?' he asks.

'What do you mean?'

'Sounds like she wants to keep going.'

He doesn't say what she's thinking. It is DJ's normal, non-committal style, but still, something in it is final. She's not coming back.

And for some reason, that leaves Lena feeling lighter. As if responsibility has been let go.

They are alone in the common dining room. The nuns have provided a simple meal for the two of them, despite their late arrival. There is soup with some bread. It is a bit stale, but the crustiness has a strong appeal after the last couple of days with little food.

She is not sure if the vow for Lent extends to visitors, so she keeps her voice low whenever she needs to say something. But most of the time it is a comfortable silence. After what they've been through, there's no need to describe it to each other. They just let it settle in, their shared situation.

After dinner is finished, she guides Kojo back down the dark corridors again. No one is around, and even if they were, she doesn't care about their judgement. Not now. She needs to be held.

She feels such a potent mix of memories and emotions. She prays that DJ is okay. Why didn't she try to get in contact with Lena before setting off again? What good are her journals and pictures when there were things left to say to each other?

She remembers the last time she saw her sister and knows now that this was the reason why she pushed so hard to come to Angola, against all better judgement. Showing up uninvited, forcing herself into a team of hardworking people still grieving about the loss of Maria. She needed to reach DJ, had a responsibility and a liability that she needed to settle. And now it may never happen.

How harsh she was at the funeral. DJ's hurt face having nothing to say in retaliation. And she remembers now that DJ never was tough with her. In the years when they lived together, and since – DJ was always striking out at others, defending against injustices and trading insults. But she was never hard on her sister, despite their differences. Shielded her from the worst, always. Lena had never fully appreciated that.

Since she's been here in Angola, other memories blend together. She can't get rid of the image in her head of Benedito's orange tub spinning in the river eddy. Avelina's hand going slack in her own. The people queueing up for their identification photographs. The burned-out shell of a home where DJ and Maria had been living together, in love and happy.

Photographs she's taken and not yet had a chance to develop. These will remain imprinted on her mind until she can get them developed in the darkroom back in London. Things will make more sense then.

There is a small and surprising feeling of relief. A pause. She has a sense that the journey might break here and just give her some time. To think about what kind of person she wants to be now, looking ahead. And who she wants with her, alongside.

They reach the end of the corridor and stand in front of her door. She pulls him into her room, looking into his eyes directly, like she couldn't do before. He raises his eyebrows with a smile and she decides she loves him for it. For everything.

She moves closer and kisses him. Gentle, then more eager and building. She stops for a moment and huddles into his embrace. He holds her without relaxing back, and she loves him more.

'Are you okay?' he asks. She holds him tighter.

After another moment he says, 'What about Lucien?'

She doesn't answer at first. Doesn't change her position.

'That's his name, isn't it? Back in London.'

'Oh,' she thinks a moment. 'That wasn't exactly true, not any more.'

He still holds her, but moves back a little to look at her face. 'You like to keep people at a distance, don't you?'

'Not always, not now.' She burrows in closer, not wanting any space between them.

He moves to kiss her neck, pulling her hair back and shifting the loose collar down. 'I've been wanting to do this since…' he says, but doesn't finish his sentence. He stops. 'Does that hurt?' He lightly touches behind her neck where the camera strap had burned a line. She shakes her head.

His face relaxes as he kisses her shoulder and then the palm of her hand. He loops a finger around the marks on her wrist where the ties were earlier that day. 'What about there?' he asks.

'No, I'm not sure why there still is a line. I guess my skin just holds onto things.'

She moves to the bed. He lets out a quiet laugh. 'You must be crazy!' he whispers. 'In a nunnery?'

'Right here, right now,' she says. 'It's needed.'

'If that's how you feel…' he says, and the kissing starts again.

'I need it,' she says between breaths, not sure if he hears. The feeling of his hands under her clothes brushing her skin makes every nerve come awake and to attention.

She wants the whole of his body touching hers. She pulls off his shirt and hers, trousers also. Must feel his skin, all of it. They turn into a fantastic braided tangle of legs and hands. Faces exploring and exclaiming astonishment at the other, like opposites in a mirror.

Him under her, she rears up her chest and her breasts feel free. His hands go to them again and again then trace down her hips and around the curves. In the darkness she can see his teeth in such a broad smile she laughs with him out loud.

I shouldn't be doing this, she thinks. Should be thinking of DJ. Praying or something.

But on a deeper level, she knows better. This is exactly what people should do when they want to feel alive. To make meaning in a senseless war. To make love, when the world seems like it has almost run out of supply.

Maria, Benedito, Avelina, her parents and everyone else along the way were preparing her for this moment. To feel the flesh, rush of blood and connection of bodies. To celebrate the life in her and in this man.

'I think I'm in love with you,' he says afterwards. He lies on his chest, looking away.

A light single bedsheet is all that covers them. The mosquito netting, a tent overhead, protects them in a safe, blurry prism.

She leans over his back in that single bed. With a light fingertip, she traces his muscles over the bones, the spine forming a perfect valley between triangular pieces. She remembers when she first saw his back, outlined by the police headlights, in the night he negotiated for Jake.

'I think I'm in love with you too.'

'I mean, I know it.'

'Me too.'

Forty-eight

You are on the move again. Such a relief, after so many days of sadness and stagnation. The air moving past, the sounds of the insects and the engine, all these are familiar, as they should be, and it's good.

You are going to the *Abençoadas*. You cannot wait. The goddesses grouped together to protect love from conflict, from everything. They will understand you, will welcome you. Absolute faith in that.

You will see your Maria again, you know that now. You were grieving before but now it is obvious. You have so much to tell her, so much you never got the chance to say. Your throat feels like it wants to burst open with it all. You want to talk and sing and shout all at once, and you do. Over the motorcycle noise, no one can hear you.

The sun is descending and you know it is reckless to be moving at this hour, but it can't be helped. You don't need to bother to scan the ground any more for landmines, nothing can stop you now. You just need to get over the border and turn west towards Lubumbashi. You can almost see the Kafue already. Turquoise waters, small encampment beside. Hear them singing and holding each other with the kind of protection and healing that only women can give.

The river will be running rapid and twisting through the green landscape. Congo – the country of tropical forests and canopies. Not like here, the dry menacing highlands, the place that threatened you and the woman you love.

No one can touch you now. After all that you have been through, you must be bullet-proof.

Don't stop, straight ahead. Mind that rock, over that bridge.

She's waiting there for you, so brilliantly, gloriously happy.

Acknowledgements

There are a great number of people who have inspired me or helped me breathe life into these ideas and then get them written down. First of all, my parents have always believed in me and supported my creativity and adventures, starting with when they bought me my first camera at the age of ten. From my first trip abroad to Nepal, to my travels for work to Kosovo, Angola, the Democratic Republic of Congo, Sudan and other places more dangerous than they wanted to know, thank you for letting me roam and not second-guessing my instincts.

To my earliest writing teachers, I owe so much for the skills of observation and harnessing the imagination: Connie Weber, Harlan Underhill, Alyce Depree and others. Later, the likes of Helena Maria Viramontes and Clare Allan, on different continents and in different decades, taught me about the discipline of writing, the beauty of language, and handling the intricacies of plot. Clare Clark was an excellent mentor to me in recent years, and I am grateful for her time and guidance.

To my early readers and friends: Tansy Hawksley, Tina Baker, Julia Silk, Flora Spiegel, Euridice Monteiro, Emily Steadman, Mimi Kyazze, Rebekah Lattin-Rawstrone, Justine Solomons and others, thank you for the frank feedback and encouragement along the way. It really helps to know that, as a writer, you are not alone on this journey.

To my publishers at Unbound: Xander Cansell, Caitlin Harvey, John Mitchinson, Anna Simpson and others: thank you for seeing the potential in my book and giving me a chance. My editors Sue Lascelles Belfrage and Mary Chesshyre both did brilliant jobs in smoothing over any rough spots and helping to make the book shine.

But I couldn't be publishing this book without my supporters, and the team who helped make the crowdfunding happen. A huge thank you to the Kyazze family members (you know who you are!) who helped me pull together the video, music, plan and outreach to make the campaign successful. And to my Patrons and Super Patrons, near and far, it was so moving to reach out to people across the world and have the connections come in like threads, tying us close together. I received pledges and wishes of support from as far away as Myanmar, Germany, East Timor, California, Italy, Kansas, Uganda, South Africa and everywhere in between. That has been truly a testimony to the power of family and friendship over decades, and to the love of books.

I would never have made it to this stage without the support of Kanatta Kyazze, a man who does not generally read novels but made an exception in my case. You are my anchor and my better half; I would not be the writer I am without you.

And to my children, who inspire me every day, and force me to squeeze my writing into the margins of trampoline practice or piano lessons and countless other obligations, I am very grateful for the lessons in efficiency. They also inspire me with their confidence and unconditional love for family and each other. I cannot take credit for much of their successes, but I do my best to learn from them. I look forward to both their efforts in life and in creative writing, taking shape already.

Unbound is the world's first crowdfunding publisher, established in 2011.

We believe that wonderful things can happen when you clear a path for people who share a passion. That's why we've built a platform that brings together readers and authors to crowdfund books they believe in – and give fresh ideas that don't fit the traditional mould the chance they deserve.

This book is in your hands because readers made it possible. Everyone who pledged their support is listed at the front of the book and below. Join them by visiting unbound.com and supporting a book today.

Pedro Almeida
Rachel Atkinson
Shola Awolesi
Shahina Bahar
Lydia Baker
Tina Baker
Jamie Balfour-Paul
Jackie Bee
Laura Biven
Uncle Joe and Aunt Edith Bookstein

Chantal Brooks
Oli Brown
Lucy Campbell
Elysa Christy
Jane Davies
Lisa Davies
Rosamund Davies
Colleen Dawson
Annemieke De Jong
Benedict Dempsey

Sarah Denness
Julie Dowling
Hubert Dupont
Ruth Dwight
Jonathan M H Ellis
Ariane Fabien
Andy Featherstone
Decorah Flett
Tracy Frankel
Emma Fulton
Matthew Geyman
Dan Glaister
Ruth Gordon
Lola Gostelow
Emma Grae
Tansy Hawksley
David Hockaday
Janet Honigmann
Zehra Jemal
Helen Jinadu
Reid Johnson
Noor Kham
Dan Kieran
W Kilroy
Eliza Koso
Dr. Jones Kyazze
Lizzie Loos
Dominique Louis
Sarah Lubischer
Yvonne MacPherson
Ed McGovern

Elisabeth Megitt
Mel Merritt
Dr. Renee Miller
John Mitchinson
Nidhi Mittal
Rebecca Moore
Carlo Navato
Joseph Nhan-O'Reilly
Maweta Odesola
Anne Partridge
Nigel Pearson
Justin Pollard
Julia Post
Hannah Reichardt
David Renton
Johanna Riley
Oscar Scafidi
Justine Solomons
Eamon Somers
Adrian Spalding
Adam Stumacher
Robert Symonds
Autumn Szeliga
Ilya Temchenko
Naomi Tiley
Ellen Tsang
Kathryn Tsibulsky
Wendy Wagler
Jessica Wallentin
Deborah Weisshaar
Danielle Woodward